"I think you don't dare open your heart again because you don't believe God uses everything for our good. Pain is all part of the chance we take when we open our hearts,"

Pilar said, touching her friend on the shoulder.

"Well, right now I don't have time for heart stuff. I haven't met anyone who is my type," Rachel responded.

"Not even Eli Cavanaugh?"

Rachel tried to ignore the little rush she felt at the mention of his name.

"I think he's very attractive, very appealing. And by the flush I can see creeping up your neck, I think you are thinking the same thing," Pilar teased.

* * *

Books by Carolyne Aarsen

Love Inspired

*Stealing Home

CAROLYNE AARSEN

and her husband, Richard, live on a small ranch in northern Alberta, where they have raised four children and numerous foster children, and are still raising cattle. Carolyne crafts her stories in her office with a large west-facing window through which she can watch the changing seasons while struggling to make her words obey.

Brought Together
By Baby

CAROLYNE
AARSEN

Steeple
Hill®

Published by Steeple Hill Books™

Special thanks and acknowledgment are given to Carolyne Aarsen for her contribution to the TINY BLESSINGS series.
This book is dedicated to caregivers of handicapped people young and old. May God bless you and give you strength for your task. May you find peace in His love and His purpose. I'd also like to thank Mindy Starns Clark for her valuable and selfless help on nonprofits and charities.

 STEEPLE HILL BOOKS

Steeple
Hill®

ISBN 0-373-87322-0

BROUGHT TOGETHER BY BABY

My grace is sufficient for you, for My power is made perfect in weakness.

—II Corinthians 12:9

Eli—Hebrew name meaning "ascended." This Old Testament figure was a high priest of Israel and instructed the young Samuel.

Rachel—Hebrew name meaning "ewe." In the Bible's Old Testament, Rachel was the favorite wife of Jacob and the mother of Joseph and Benjamin.

Grace—A Latin and English name meaning "lovely or graceful, a virtue."

Chapter One

"I'll speak to LaReese Binet about where she'd like her donation to go myself, Reuben." Rachel Noble tucked her papers into her briefcase, one eye on the clock hanging on the wood-paneled wall of her office. "I don't have time to talk now. I'm due for dinner at my parents' place in twenty minutes." She frowned as her assistant launched into a litany of complaints, then cut him off. "Just let me know if she calls again." She hung up, picked up her cell phone and dropped it into her briefcase along with the small gift she had bought for little Gracie, a penance for not visiting her newly adopted sister more often. The offices and hallways of the Noble Foundation were quiet as Rachel hurried down to the parking garage.

Her mother's weekly invitation to the Noble plantation had included the warning to dress casually. Her mother was always nagging her to cut loose and relax. Rachel glanced at her dove-gray tailored suit and peach silk blouse. Her mother would have to take her as she was. She didn't have time to go home and change.

When Rachel returned to Richmond after a five-year absence, her parents had begged her to move back onto the plantation with them. But Rachel had been on her own too long. Instead she had opted for a modern condo west of Main Street. Though she was seldom home, it suited her.

She stopped behind an SUV at a four-way stop, trying not to tap her manicured nails on her steering wheel as the driver in front of her let car after car go by. It looked like she would have time to speak with Reuben after all.

Rachel stiffened, as a motorcycle pulled up beside her. Its obscene roar drowned out the gentle Brahms symphony coming from her car's CD player.

The driver stopped. He straddled the motorcycle, easily holding it up as he waited. He wore a denim jacket, blue jeans and cowboy boots.

Rachel clenched the steering wheel. She hated motorcycles. If Keith had been driving his truck that night—

She pushed the futile thoughts about her late fiancé aside. That was in the past. Over.

In spite of that, she couldn't seem to avoid giving the man on the motorcycle a quick glance.

He pushed his helmet back and, as she caught his eye, a slow smile crept over his mouth, making the corners of his eyes crinkle. Wisps of blond hair curled out from the front of his helmet, framing a lean face.

She looked ahead, angry with her flicker of reaction to his lazy good looks.

As she made the turn leading to her parents' home, the biker roared past her, leaving her frustrated and with unwelcome memories.

She ejected the CD, found a radio station that played classic rock and turned up the volume. As she drove, she focused on the work that she had to do tomorrow. The jobs that needed her attention. She had to leave the past in the past.

By the time she turned onto her parents' tree-shaded drive, she felt back in control again. The evening was going to be just fine.

She steered her car through a narrow opening between two rows of clipped shrubs that surrounded the main house, pulling up in front of a converted four-car garage.

And her heart flipped over.

The motorcycle that had zipped past her now stood parked on the inlaid brick drive in front of the garage, a helmet hanging from the handlebars.

Great.

She took a long slow breath, just as her yoga instructor had taught her. Focused on the now, the present.

She picked up Gracie's gift and walked with careful, deliberate steps up the brick paved drive to the front door. Maybe the motorcycle belonged to a deliveryman. Or one of the maid's boyfriends.

Her parents' visitor was most likely coming later.

As she stepped inside the door, Aleeda, the housekeeper, swept down the square rigged flying staircase toward her carrying an armful of linens.

"Well, well. You're back again," she said, smiling at Rachel. "Your mother is in the kitchen, concocting…" She shrugged. "Something."

"Thanks for the warning, Aleeda. Do you have any idea what she plans to feed me?"

"They've got company." Aleeda gave her a mysterious smile. "So I think she'll be doing something more traditional for you and their guest." Aleeda gave her a quick nod, and then strode off to the back of the house before Rachel could ask her who it was that had arrived on that dreadful motorcycle.

Rachel caught her reflection in the mirror hanging in the front hall and took a moment to smooth a wayward strand of chestnut-brown hair back from her forehead. All neat and tidy, she thought. The dark lashes fringing her hazel eyes didn't need mascara. Her cheeks were, well, pale. But so be it.

She whisked one hand down her skirt as she walked along the narrow hallway toward the kitchen, brushing away the few wrinkles she had gotten from driving.

Her mother stood at the huge counter that served as an island in the modernized kitchen, her knife flashing as she chopped vegetables. She wore a bright orange, loose, woven shirt over a wildly patterned silk T-shirt in hues of turquoise, orange, red and gold that accented her short chestnut-brown hair, worn in a spiky style. The kitchen table, tucked away in a plant-laden nook, was set with her mother's earthenware dishes. Definitely casual.

"Ah. There you are." Beatrice put down her knife and swept around the island, arms spread out, her shirt and matching skirt flowing out behind her. She enveloped her daughter in a warm hug, holding her close. "I'm so glad you came. And right on time." She drew away, cupping Rachel's face in her narrow hands, her hazel eyes traveling over her. "You're looking a little pale, my dear. Have you been taking your kelp supplements?"

Rachel lifted her hand in a vague gesture. "I've been busy…" She laid the present for Gracie on the counter.

"Honey, honey, honey." Beatrice shook her head in admonition. "You have to take care of yourself. Your body is a temple of the Holy Spirit. God needs healthy servants to do His work on earth."

Rachel merely smiled. She wasn't going to get into a discussion with her mother over what God needed or didn't need. For the past eight years she had put God out of her life. Or tried to. Now and again glimpses of Him would come through, but she generally managed to ignore them. She preferred her independence, and God required too much and gave too little.

Beatrice slipped her arm around Rachel's shoulders and drew her toward the counter. "Your father and I have a lovely surprise for you. Gracie's pediatrician said he would come and visit us."

"He's here now?"

Beatrice nodded, giving her daughter a sly grin. "I thought you might want to meet him."

A moment of awareness dawned. "Is he the fool on the motorcycle?"

Beatrice frowned and tapped her fingers on her daughter's shoulders. "Rachel Augusta Charlene Noble, you shouldn't use words like that. Especially about someone as wonderful as Eli."

Rachel had hoped that adopting not-yet-two-year-old Gracie would satisfy her mother's deep-rooted desire for grandchildren. Well, this was one romance she was going to nip in the bud. "I'm sorry, Mom, but as far as I'm concerned, anyone who drives a motorcycle isn't firing on all cylinders. *Especially* if he's a pediatrician." Rachel picked a baby carrot from the bowl sitting on the counter and took a bite. "Where's Dad?"

"He and the estimable Dr. Eli are out in the garden with Gracie. I do believe they're coming back now."

Rachel wandered over to the window overlooking the grounds, popping the last of the carrot in her mouth. A tall, narrow-hipped man sauntered alongside her father, the tips of his fingers pushed into the front pockets of his blue jeans, his softly worn shirt flowing over broad shoulders. He reached over and feathered a curl of Gracie's hair back from her face, smiling softly at her. Gracie laughed up at him and snuggled closer to her father.

Rachel couldn't mesh the picture with the one she had created of Gracie's Dr. Eli. Until her mother's pronouncement, she had always pictured the man her parents spoke so highly of as an older, portly gentleman, not this…cowboy.

Who drove a motorcycle.

A chill drifted over Rachel and she spun away from the window.

"And what are you making for dinner?" she asked, looking for a distraction.

When Rachel was younger, her mother had hardly darkened the doorway of the kitchen except to give Francine, their cook for the past fifteen years, directions on when to serve which course. But in the past few years, Beatrice had started exploring various culinary options and had settled on macrobiotic cooking. The result was that Francine turned up her nose at what Beatrice wanted to make and had quit and been re-hired a number of times. The two of them had settled on part-time work, which suited Francine just fine and gave Beatrice the space she needed to create her concoctions.

Beatrice looked up from the salad she was working with her hands. "Polenta with corn, herbed black soybeans, carrots and broccoli with ume dill dressing and a pressed Chinese cabbage salad."

Rachel thought of the fast-food outlets she had passed on her way over here and her stomach growled.

"Francine made sure there was herbed chicken for you, Gracie and Eli, and she made your favorite chocolate cake for dessert." Her mother gave her a quick smile. "I know how much you love your empty calories. That's why you're so pale, you know."

"I'm fine, Mother." Rachel ate another carrot as if to show Beatrice that she knew how to make healthy choices.

"Is that my little girl?" Charles called out affectionately.

Rachel looked back over her shoulder just as her father burst into the room. He strode to her side, and gave her a quick one-armed hug, balancing his youngest daughter on the other arm.

"Hello, Dad," she said, leaning against him. "Good to see you."

She glanced at Gracie, who grinned at her, her curly brown hair framing a heart-shaped face. She wore blue jean overalls today with a soft pink T-shirt. Fairly normal considering her mother's personal taste in clothing.

"Hey, there," Rachel said with a quick smile, stroking her sister's shoulder. Gracie held her arms out to Rachel, overbalanced, and tried to compensate, her movements jerky. Rachel restored her back to her father's arms but took a step away from them.

Gracie was adorable, cute and loving. But every time Rachel was around her, she felt inadequate and, quite frankly, a little nervous.

It hadn't helped that the first time Rachel saw the girl that had captured her parents' hearts the child had been attached to a respirator, monitor, IV and other machines. Gracie had cerebral palsy and had been recovering from a bad seizure. Her parents had just applied to adopt her. So they had asked Rachel to come with them to meet her.

Rachel had thought she'd overcome her hatred of hospitals, but five minutes of standing by Gracie's bedside was all she could take. The hiss of the respirator and the pervasive scent of disinfectant broke over her in a wave of angry memories and nausea.

She gave her parents her blessing and left as soon as she could.

Since then, every time she saw the girl, she saw helplessness and sickness and hospitals. And she felt uncomfortable.

"Here, little one, I brought you a present." Rachel offered the toddler the wrapped box as a peace offering.

"What do you say, honey?" Charles prompted.

"Hank you." Gracie said with a proud grin at her father.

Charles tried to catch Rachel's gaze, but she looked away. She knew her father didn't always understand her reaction to her adorable little sister. Rachel didn't always, either. But there it was.

Charles looked behind him at the man she knew had been watching them. "Rachel, I'd like you to meet Dr. Eli. He is Gracie's pediatrician. Eli, this is our daughter, Rachel."

"I believe we've already met," Eli said, the same lazy smile crooking his mouth as he held out his hand to her.

She gave him a polite smile. She could do that much. It wasn't his fault that her parents were itching to be inlaws. "The motorcycle man."

"That's me." His hand was warm, his fingers long, and at his touch she felt a flicker of awareness that had been dormant for a long time now.

She didn't like it.

"I'm surprised that you ride one," she said, unable to stop the defensive note from creeping into her voice. "You being a doctor and all."

"And all what?" His grin mocked her comment.

It was an overreaction, but she couldn't seem to help herself. "And all the responsibility you carry," she added. "What if something happened to you?"

"It's cheap transportation. And I'm careful."

"Famous last words," she said with a chill in her voice.

His sea-green eyes held her gaze, his head angled to one side as if trying to figure her out. Well, he could try all he wanted. The only time their paths might cross again would be at a Noble Foundation fund-raiser for the hospital. He didn't need to know more about her than her name.

"We can eat," Beatrice announced, taking Gracie from her husband's arms. "Why don't we unwrap your present when we have dessert," she said to Gracie, setting the gift aside. "Rachel, you get your usual spot. Eli, you can sit across from her."

Beatrice shepherded them all toward the cozy eating nook whose floor-to-ceiling windows overlooked the kitchen garden. Rachel sat in "her" chair, noticing the place setting.

When the Nobles first moved to Chestnut Grove from their old home, Rachel and her mother had gone touring the local market. Rachel stopped at a booth that displayed brightly colored earthenware dishes, each place setting unique. Her mother insisted that Rachel choose one for each of them and a couple for her aunt, uncle and cousin. The dishes only came out on family occasions, never when they had company.

Rachel gave her mother a quick glance now, recognizing the not-so-light hint her mother was giving her. At any other time she might have been amused, but Eli and his irresponsible motorcycle had unnerved her.

Beatrice suddenly busied herself buckling Gracie into her specially made high chair, making sure she was comfortable.

"This looks lovely, Beatrice," Charles said, holding out his hand to his daughter on one side, Eli on the other. "We usually say grace before our meal," he explained to Eli.

"That's fine with me. So do the Cavanaughs."

That seemed an odd way to talk about his family, but Rachel didn't have time to wonder. Her father had squeezed her hand, and she bowed her head as he began to·pray.

She heard her father talking to God, but couldn't join in on his heartfelt prayer. Though she had been born and raised with faith, she had drifted away over the past few years. She didn't need God, or what He supposedly offered her and she knew He certainly didn't need her. Her parents weren't happy with her choices, but she was thankful they kept their distance. And probably prayed over her.

"Help yourself, Eli," Beatrice said when Charles was done. "We don't stand on formality here. The only rule we have is start with what's in front of you and pass it to the right."

"And finish what's on my plate, I imagine," Eli said with a quick grin at Beatrice.

"If you can," Rachel muttered, grimacing at the bowl set nearest to her.

"Don't pay attention to the carnivore," Beatrice said, fluttering her hands in dismissal of Rachel's comment. "In spite of being raised with gourmet cooking, Rachel's idea of a well-balanced diet is cake in one hand and a burger in the other. I pity the man she ends up marrying."

"Well, it's a good thing I don't have a man," Rachel said with a warning glance at her mother as she passed on the bowl of soybeans. "Or any intention of getting one."

"As you said, famous last words, my dear," Beatrice threw back, unfazed by Rachel's pronouncement. "One day you'll swap that impersonal condo of yours for a house with a yard like Eli's. A nice cozy colonial." Beatrice turned to the doctor. "I understand that you're in the process of fixing it up?"

"Actually, my brother Ben has been working on it. He's the carpenter." Eli took a small helping of what looked like corn with a pained expression that made Rachel smile in spite of herself. "He's been nagging at me to make some decisions about the kitchen, but I'm not sure if I want to go modern or stay with the colonial theme."

"Rachel might be able to help you there," Charles said, ignoring the prod of Rachel's foot, beaming at Eli like he was already a favored son. "She's very good at interior decorating."

Rachel didn't know where that had come from. Her parents didn't like the eclectic mix of masks, rugs and memorabilia from her many trips that graced her condo. Said it made her place look like a museum, not a home.

"I know what I want. My biggest problem, however, seems to be finding time to make the decisions," Eli said, glancing at Rachel as if he too understood what was going on.

"No woman pushing you to get done?" Charles asked.

Rachel gave her father a harder nudge.

Which he also ignored.

She shot her mother a warning glance to make sure she didn't join in. But her mother was trying to coax some food into Gracie, who sat in her chair, back rigid, lips pressed together.

"I'm not ready for a woman yet" was all Eli said.

Rachel was thankful when the conversation moved on to traffic downtown, the changing pace of life, and a smattering of politics, and then to some of the fund-raising activities the Noble organization had been involved in.

"There's the annual Noble Foundation picnic coming up soon. You'll have to make sure to attend," Beatrice said, carefully lifting Gracie out of her high chair. "Rachel takes care of it and has it here, on the plantation."

"You make it sound like I do it single-handedly," Rachel admonished her mother. "I have a large staff that does a lot of work, as well."

"But you don't delegate enough. I thought hiring those two assistants to replace Anita would ease your workload, but if anything, you are even busier."

"They're still so new, Mom. I can't just hand them the files and expect them to deal with all of it."

"They *are* well trained."

"They need just a bit more experience." She gave her mother another warning look. They did not need to discuss this in front of a complete stranger.

"I love you dear, but I also know you," Beatrice said, as if ignoring Rachel's warning, "and you have to stop thinking you can control everything. Sometimes you have to let go and let God."

"I don't want to delegate to Him, either," Rachel muttered. "Can we change the subject?"

Beatrice only sighed, smoothing Gracie's hair. "Do you want to hold Gracie?" she asked.

Rachel glanced at the toddler who lay passive in her mother's arms. This was not a subject she was comfortable with, either. She knew she should accept, but she was scared she'd do something wrong.

"She won't hurt you," Eli said quietly, as if sensing her apprehension.

His comment hung between them.

Then in her peripheral vision she saw Gracie twitch. The child's arms splayed out, her legs became rigid. She gave a pathetic little wail.

"Gracie. C'mon, girlie." Beatrice tried to make her sit, but she wouldn't. Or couldn't.

Rachel's heart jumped in her chest at the sight of the girl's head thrown back and her body stiff.

"Massage her legs. It looks like a muscle spasm," Eli said, his voice calm, in control. He squatted beside Beatrice, demonstrating.

Beatrice did what he said, and Rachel breathed a sigh of relief as Gracie's body slowly relaxed.

"See? Not that bad."

"No. I was a bit frightened, though." Beatrice glanced at Rachel. "You can hold her now."

Rachel's pager buzzed at her waist and she couldn't stop the twinge of relief. Reuben to her rescue.

Chapter Two

Rachel gave her mother an apologetic smile. "Sorry, Mom. I have to take this call. Excuse me, Dad. Eli." Thankful for the distraction, she strode down the hallway to her father's den to use the phone there in private.

"Talk to me," she said as soon as Reuben picked up.

"LaReese Binet changed her mind again."

Rachel tapped her fingernail against her teeth as her mind scrambled around this new problem.

"She said she wants to see us tonight," Reuben continued. "In fact, you should have been there about five minutes ago, but I knew you were at your parents' place and I held off as long as I dared."

"That's okay, you weren't interrupting much. Polenta, ume dill dressing, matchmaking and Gracie." She shuddered slightly as she remembered the sound of her sister's helpless cry. She admired her parents for taking this child in. She knew she couldn't have done it.

"Pardon me?"

"Never mind. What is the problem now?"

"Mrs. Binet wants to see the quarterly statements of the Barnabas Society. Wants to make sure they're on the up-and-up."

"They'll see that as an insult." The Barnabas Society was a network of older Southern belles who had been around since after Reconstruction. Well established, well endowed, they had set up a camp for inner-city children, but never said no to extra dollars. Though not at any cost. They did have their Southern pride after all.

"I've been in touch with the director. Said he'll see what he can do."

"I really don't know how good a match the donor and recipient are in this case." Rachel tugged on her earlobe, pacing the carpet. "LaReese likes control but so does Barnabas."

A faint knock at the door of the study interrupted her train of thought. Frowning, she glanced up. "Yes?"

Eli stood in the doorway, filling it with his height. "Your mother asked me to tell you that they'll be serving cake and coffee in the gazebo."

"Thank you. I'll be with you all in a couple of minutes." She gave him a tight smile, feeling suddenly awkward. They hadn't started off on the right foot and that scene with Gracie hadn't helped.

But he turned on his heel and strode away before she had a chance. It shouldn't have bothered her, but she had a vague sense of discomfort.

She turned her attention back to Reuben, wondering why she cared what Gracie's attractive pediatrician thought of her. "Tell Mrs. Binet that I'll be by in…" She glanced quickly at the grandfather clock in the corner of her father's study. "About forty-five minutes."

"I hate to pressure you, Rachel, but could you make it sooner?"

"That *is* sooner. My goodness, Reuben, she lives right on the edge of Winchester Park. I'll be lucky to get there that soon by the time I've parked and walked up to her condo," Rachel said. "I just have to say goodbye to my parents. And then I'll be on the road."

"Okay, then. I'll probably be there when you arrive."

Rachel pressed the button to end the call, biting her lip. Her parents wouldn't be happy, but there was nothing she could do about it. LaReese Binet was too important to the Foundation. She was a regular contributor and a part of Rachel's network whenever she needed to pad out a guest list for celebrity events.

LaReese had come into a great deal of money when her husband died and had already been approached by every possible organization that could find her number and pester her. If Rachel did not handle this woman exactly right, LaReese could easily decamp and end up giving her money to the smoothest-talking charlatan that came down the pike.

And there were enough of them. It made Rachel's blood boil every time she heard of organizations that seemed legitimate but ended up taking up to eighty percent of their client's money in so-called "administration fees."

Her parents were already sitting in the gazebo, tall cups of iced tea on the wicker and glass table in front of them, when Rachel rejoined them. Gracie was playing on a large blanket at their feet, looking content and perfectly normal. She smiled up at Rachel, her light brown eyes sparkling in the early evening light. She was adorable—that much Rachel had to concede.

"Excuse me, Mom, Dad, Dr. Cavanaugh." Her eyes grazed Eli, who was lounging in his wicker chair, swirling the ice cubes in his glass, looking too much at home. "I'm sorry, but I'll have to excuse myself. Reuben just called. We have an emergency with one of our clients."

"Oh, honey, why don't you let him take care of it?" Beatrice turned to her husband. "Charles, talk to her."

Charles simply shrugged and smiled up at his daughter. "I wish you could stay, dear. We don't get to see you very often. Gracie hardly knows you."

"Besides, I have chocolate cake that Francine made just for you," Beatrice added, her voice taking on a petulant tone. "You know your father and I don't eat that kind of thing."

"I'm really sorry, Mom, and I'd love to have some cake but—"

"I'll pack some up for you." Beatrice slipped out of her chair, waving at the men to stay in their seats. "I'll be back in a flash."

Rachel surreptitiously eased the cuff of her shirt up to catch a glimpse of her watch. She had given herself enough time to say goodbye, but at this rate she would have to risk a speeding ticket to get to LaReese's place on time. As she shrugged her shirt into place, she caught Eli watching her, a half smile tugging on his lips. She held his gaze as if challenging his humor, but he didn't even blink, or look away. Rachel wasn't used to that. Most men were intimidated by her. And she liked to keep it that way.

"I heard that you've been talking to LaReese Binet," her father was saying.

Rachel pulled her attention back to her father, taken aback by his words. Had she spoken LaReese's name aloud?

"Oh, don't get all confidential on me," Charles said with a huge laugh. "Phillip Thewlis told me at the fifteenth hole at the new golf course." He frowned. "Or maybe it was the fourteenth. I remember he was working his way out of the sand trap and I believe that's on the fifteenth—no, wait…"

Don't tap your foot. Don't fidget.

Charles snapped his fingers. "What am I thinking of—it was the twelfth hole." He shook his head as if surprised at his own foolishness. "Phillip heard from LaReese's beloved nephew that she was eager to redeem herself by giving away a bit of the money she inherited when her husband died."

Rachel would hardly call 2.3 million dollars "a bit" of money. That's why the personal hand holding. LaReese had been making noises about putting her money into other places, and right now the Noble Foundation needed dollars if they were going to be able to fulfill all the requests they had earmarked for funding.

"Can't buy redemption, you know," Charles said sadly. "I would like to tell her that. God's love and sacrifice are the greatest free gifts known, or unknown in many cases, to man."

Impatience with her father's sermonizing flashed through Rachel, and right behind it, shame. Her father was sincere in his faith. That she didn't share it wasn't his fault. In fact, there was the occasional moment when she wished she shared his trust in God.

She glanced at Eli, wondering if her father's easy mention of God created discomfort in him as well.

He was looking down at his hands, his expression serious as he rubbed the fingers of one hand over the back of the other, again and again. It was then she noticed the long jagged scar that ran from the knuckle of his pinky to the base of his thumb. It was white and puckered, as if it had been poorly stitched. She wondered if he'd gotten it riding his motorcycle.

At that moment he looked up at her, giving her a languid look that she was sure most women would find a challenge. She just found it annoying.

"Here's your cake, dear." Beatrice held out a large foam container.

"This is half of it," Rachel exclaimed, weighing it in her hand.

"Your father and I won't eat it—you may as well take it home."

"Looks like chocolate cake is on the menu for my next few meals."

"Honey, no." Beatrice frowned and was about to take it away from her.

"No, you don't." Rachel winked at her mother as she pulled the container out of reach. "Don't worry. I'm just kidding. I'll have a piece tonight and take the rest to work. I'm sure Reuben and Lorna will be fighting over it."

"Just make sure you do that," Beatrice warned. "Now give me a kiss and you better get going."

Rachel gave her mother a quick hug and a kiss, then bent over to do the same with Charles and Gracie.

Before she left, Rachel risked a glance at Eli. Her cheeks warmed when his eyes snagged hers. He was fifty feet away, but even across that distance his gaze felt as real as a touch.

As she walked to her car she shook the feeling off. Basic chemistry. That was all. He was good looking; they were both single.

Only, she wasn't looking. She thought she'd made that clear to her parents when she moved back here. Guess it was time for the classic mother-daughter chat. In reverse.

Rachel stifled a yawn as she opened the file of the next item on the agenda. The meeting last night with LaReese Binet had taken too long and yielded too little.

"And how are we sitting on the dream home program for the children's hospital?" she asked Lorna as she glanced through the file. The Noble Foundation took care of some of the hospital's fund-raising activities, and next to the annual celebrity dinner and ball, this was their premier fund-raiser.

"I've got the mock-ups done on the brochures." Lorna Kirkpatrick laid the papers on the low cherry-wood table between them. "The construction company was concerned about the placement of the name and logo, so I modified it. I hope it's what you want."

Rachel glanced over the brochure, frowning as she leaned back in the leather couch. "This blue is too flat." Rachel circled the block of color behind the lettering, "And I'd like this yellow intensified. I'll call them and let them know."

"Why don't you let me take care of that?" Lorna said.

"Thanks, Lorna, but I know exactly what I want to see." Lorna nodded, but Rachel could see she wasn't happy with the decision.

"Anything else you want me to do for now?" Lorna asked.

"You can see how Zoe and Hamilton are doing with the fund-raising for Nagy's golf tournament. See if they need some help."

Rachel laid her the papers with the changes on them on her desk and turned to Reuben as Lorna left the office. He didn't look as if he had spent most of last night over endless cups of coffee convincing a finicky, elderly lady to wait with her donation while they did some background work on her charity of the day. "I imagine it's a bit early to expect anything from you, Reuben."

"Au contraire." Reuben bent over and pulled a sheaf of papers out of his leather briefcase. "This is rough for now, but I printed this off their Web site…" He handed them to her. "I did some phoning around and got this from a source." More papers. "And I had a personal chat with the head of the organization just before the meeting."

Where did he get his energy? Rachel got tired just thinking about all he had accomplished after their meeting with LaReese.

"This is great, Reuben. Our next step is to check their charitable donation status and, if we can, get a copy of their mission statement and do some deeper background work on them."

"Consider it done." Reuben flashed a smile. "And while I'm at it, I thought I would check out a couple of other possible places, just to see what might interest her. Lorna has been looking, as well."

Rachel frowned at him. "If LaReese gives her money to the Foundation, we have more than enough places that the money can go. I would like us to work with what we have. We'll connect again as necessary."

As Rachel pushed herself up from the couch, taking a moment to button up her suit jacket, Lorna buzzed her. Her mother was on the line.

"Thanks again, Reuben," Rachel said before she picked

up the handset. "For someone who has come on board only recently, you have done exceptional work."

He gave her a nod, then turned and strode out of the office.

Rachel walked around her desk to drop into the large leather chair behind it. "Hello, Mother," she said into the phone, "what can I do for you?"

"So businesslike."

"Considering it's your business I'm running, you should be pleased." Rachel spun her chair around, looking out over the skyline of Chestnut Grove.

"Honey, I'm always pleased with you. You know that."

"The chocolate cake was really good. Reuben and Lorna send their thanks."

"I'm glad to know you shared it. But I have a favor to ask of you. Your grandfather wants us to come to Vermont in a couple of weeks, but I don't dare take Gracie along quite yet. Would you be willing to baby-sit?"

Rachel clutched the phone. Willing? Maybe. Capable? No. "When would that be?" she asked, turning around to check her appointment book. *Please let there be a conflict. Please.*

"The last weekend of the month."

Bingo. Charity fund-raiser. Big deal. Big celebrities. "Sorry, Mom. I'm booked up."

"Oh, dear. That was the only weekend your grandfather can have us." She sighed lightly. "And I can't leave Gracie with just anybody. She's too fragile yet."

So why would you leave her with me?

"Why don't you talk to Dr. Eli about your predicament," Rachel suggested. "Surely he could recommend a private nursing agency or something similar?"

"Eli stressed that Gracie stay with someone familiar, especially because Gracie's natural mother was so casual with her care."

She shouldn't feel guilty, Rachel thought. It wasn't her idea that her parents take this child on. And it wasn't her fault that Gracie made her feel incompetent and helpless. Two feelings she had promised herself she would never allow to take over her life again.

"However, if you can't take care of her, then you can't," her mother continued. "I'm sure Eli would know where we could bring Gracie."

"I'm sure he would," Rachel agreed, relief flooding her.

"And what did you think of Dr. Eli? He's such a pleasant man. So good with Gracie."

"He seemed very nice." Now was the time to make it clear to her mother that her matchmaking wouldn't work. "But he's not my type."

"What did you say?"

The innocent tone of her mother's voice almost fooled her. "The matchmaking stuff. Mom, please. You know I don't have time for anyone right now."

"You didn't have time for anyone in the past eight years. You don't have much of a social life. All you do is work."

Rachel frowned, rocking her chair a little harder. "I need this work, Mom." It was what gave her life direction. And it was a good direction.

"What about your relationship with the Lord? Does that get pushed aside for your work, too?"

"Mother, what I do is all about helping the needy, the helpless. The very things that Jesus wants us to do on this earth." Rachel knew the right words that would appease her mother and she used them shamelessly.

"Works without faith is dead, dear."

Check. Her mother may come across as eccentric at times, but when it came to her faith, Beatrice had all the intelligence and knew all the strategies.

"This is what I do, Mother," Rachel said finally. "I don't have time for a boyfriend and I don't have the inclination for one. So please, no more awkward dinners."

She hoped her mother's silence meant that she had surrendered.

"I'm happy, Mom." She pressed on, determined to make her mother see the light. "I live a busy, active life that has purpose and meaning. I have friends and I have a community and a job that is important. And I have you and Dad and Gracie. I don't need more."

"Okay. I'm sorry. It's just that I thought you and Eli would hit it off. He's a good, kind man."

Rachel thought of the smirk she'd caught on his face. The appeal of his languid good looks. *Good* and *kind* were not words that came to mind in connection with Gracie's pediatrician.

"Well, I'm sure he'll make someone a wonderful husband. But not me, Mom."

Beatrice sighed. "Point taken, my dear. I'm sorry if I offended you."

"You created an awkward situation. But you didn't offend me."

"Good. Well, I'd better go. I have an appointment with a physical therapist and after that Dr. Eli. Shall I tell him you said hello?"

Her mother was irrepressible. "Do whatever you want, Mom. Love you." Though she said the words automatically, she did mean them. Her mother could make her crazy at times, could embarrass her at other times, but Rachel loved her parents dearly.

"Love you, too, dear."

Rachel couldn't help but smile when she hung up the phone. Dear Mom. Rachel had thought her mother's adopting Gracie would satisfy her nesting instinct, but it looked like Rachel was going to have to be on her guard.

"Okay, guys. Final play of the game and we can't afford to lose." Alex crouched down, his back to the opposing team, and sketched the play in the grass in front of Eli and the other two teammates. "Eli, Ben is going to be watching you and we want to use that. See if you can fake him out." When he was done, he held up his fist, his deep brown eyes sparkling with fun. The guys in the circle around him all hit it, called "break" and jogged to where a handkerchief on the grass of the park showed the line of scrimmage.

For the past three years, Sunday mornings would find Eli, his brother Ben, and their friends lining up against one another in Winchester Park for their weekly touch football game. Sometimes the wives and girlfriends came, sometimes they stayed at home. Sometimes Eli's pager would go off and the game would be called. Sometimes Ben's daughter Olivia would get tired and want to go home. But mostly they managed to finish their games.

The one constant was that Ben and Eli consistently played on opposing teams. It was a vague throwback to when they were young and constantly in competition with each other. Growing up had eased the competition, but hadn't erased it.

Eli unbuttoned his shirt and wiped the sweat from his

forehead with one end, squinting up at the sky, hazed over with humidity and heat. If he'd known it was going to be this warm, he wouldn't have worn blue jeans.

"Hey, Doc, I'm watchin' you." Ben grinned at Eli and nodded. "I know you have a plan."

Eli crouched down, resting his hands on his knees. "You do that, Ben. Don't think we're not counting on that."

"You're workin' me, Eli. Playin' me."

"Now, Ben. Don't be so mistrustful. Do what you think is right." He leaned a little closer. "Use the force, Luke."

Alex called out the play, and Eli could see doubt clouding Ben's face as Alex glanced down the line away from Eli. As he did, Eli broke away, and Ben took the bait and veered away from him. Eli turned, and Alex spun in a different direction and snapped the ball directly to Eli, who caught it against his chest, cradling it like a child, grinning at Ben's shout of disappointment.

Eli ran past the stroller that marked off the goal line, and spun around, holding up the ball in a gesture of victory. Ben was coming at him, vengeance in his eyes.

With a laugh, Eli swung left to avoid his brother. He looked up and, too late, saw Rachel Noble coming directly at him. She had veered off the walking path, a soft leather briefcase slung over her shoulder, cell phone clamped to one ear, a sheaf of papers in her free hand.

They would have collided, but at the last possible moment, Eli dropped his football and caught her by the shoulders to steady her and catch his balance. Her papers fell out of her hands and her briefcase slid down her shoulder as she came to an abrupt halt, teetering. She almost dropped her cell phone, as well, but it bobbled in her hands and she managed to hang on.

"What are you—?" She yanked the strap of her brief-case up her shoulder, but it stopped when it hit his hand. "Are you crazy?" She looked down at her papers. Hitched her strap up again. Hit his hand again.

Then looked up at him.

As her hazel eyes met his, anger snapping in their depths, he felt it again. A light flutter, somewhere in the region of his heart. He had experienced it when he pulled up beside her at the stop sign and she had looked over at him. And felt it again at her parents' place when he and Charles had come into the kitchen and he realized the beautiful woman he'd been openly flirting with, moments before, was his patient's sister. Daughter of one of the wealthiest families in Chestnut Grove.

She wore another suit today. This one was olive green with a white shirt. Tidy. Together. With a hint of uptight. He wondered what she would look like in blue jeans, with her hair down.

She blinked once, and to his surprise, the anger seeped out of her eyes. If she hadn't looked down, he could have seen what replaced it.

"Excuse me, please," she mumbled, pulling back against his hands.

He had forgotten he was still holding her. He released her, reluctantly.

"Sorry. I didn't see you." His apology sounded half-hearted even to him. "I was just trying to avoid Ben here." He glanced back over his shoulder at his brother, who had kept his distance but was watching the two of them with avid interest.

"That's okay. I was off the path." She was about to bend down to pick up her papers.

"Here. I'll do that." He gathered them up, but as he handed them to her he belatedly saw the dark smudge marks his fingers had left on the white sheets.

As she tried to brush them off, he realized he had left the same marks on her suit coat. "Sorry about that," he said, pointing to the faint marks of four fingers on her upper arms. "I'll pay for the cleaning."

"Please, don't worry." She gave him a quick smile that revived that flutter again. "It was my fault."

Eli rubbed the back of his neck, aware that his unbuttoned shirt hung open. He lowered his arms, tucking his hands in the front pockets of his blue jeans. He angled his chin toward her papers, feeling uncharacteristically self-conscious. "Do you work every day of the week?"

Rachel frowned up at him. "I do what needs to be done. My work is very important." Her voice took on a chill that made him take a step away.

"Of course." *Brilliant, Cavanaugh. You won the football game, but here and now you're officially a loser.* "Well, I'll see you around, I guess."

"I guess." She gave him a polite smile, and with that she became again the aloof woman that had sat across from him at Charles and Beatrice Noble's table.

"You still there, Rachel?" A man's tinny voice called out from the cell phone she still held. And without another glance at him, Rachel continued her interrupted phone conversation.

"I was at LaReese's place and thought I'd slip across the park to Bernie McNamara," she was saying. She glanced up at Eli, and for a moment he felt it again. A subtle connection.

Then she turned and started walking away, still talking. Still working.

He must have imagined it.

As Eli watched her go, Ben came up beside him. "Very nice, Eli. But I thought your life plan didn't include women for at least another year."

"Two years," Eli corrected, bending over to retrieve the football. "And even then the plan doesn't include spoiled, haughty women." Eli grinned at his brother and handed him the ball. "My life plan is firmly intact."

"Pay down your loan, buy a house, the right car, and then look for someone to share your neat, orderly life." Ben tapped Eli on the chest with a football, his expression turning serious. "Beware of plans, my brother. They have a way of flipping you midstream."

Eli didn't reply to that. He knew his brother was talking about the pain he and his daughter Olivia suffered when Ben lost his wife, Julia, to cancer.

Eli knew from personal experience that life didn't always cooperate. At one time he had a girlfriend and other plans. But the girlfriend's parents were leery of the question mark hanging over Eli's life. Eli had been adopted at age six by the Cavanaughs and the only thing he knew about his natural parents were their names, Darlene and Zeke Fulton. The last memory he had of them was a car spinning out of control, a horrifying crash and then his own life turned topsy-turvy. When the girlfriend's parents convinced her to break up with Eli, he was determined that the only way he would enter another relationship was if his own life was in order. So he made a plan and stuck to it.

But as he followed his brother back to the game, Eli threw a glance over his shoulder.

Rachel was looking back at him, as well.

Chapter Three

Rachel surveyed the homey interior of the Starlight Diner, looking for her friends Pilar Estes, Meg Kierney and Anne Smith.

She had rushed through her interview with Bernie hoping to get here on time. It had been a while since she and her friends had been able to get together for brunch and they had lots of catching up to do.

"You looking for the girls?" Sandra Lange, the owner of the diner, met Rachel at the door, her blond hair worn in its usual teased up-do. She was tying on her apron. "I just got back from church myself, but I believe that Miranda put them in the far corner, by the window."

"Thanks, Sandra." Rachel paused before joining her friends, noting Sandra's drawn features. "How have you been doing?"

"Oh, not too badly," Sandra said, with a smile. "I have to go to the cancer clinic again and the doctor will tell me what I can expect. I'm just thankful for each day God gives me. And thankful that the wheels of God grind slowly, but they do grind and each movement brings me closer to the truth."

She was talking in puzzles, but Rachel sensed that she wouldn't get more out of Sandra right now. The difficulties Sandra had faced in her life had created strength of character that many people underestimated. "I'm glad that you have your faith, Sandra."

"It's not just faith, Rachel. It's a relationship with a loving Father."

Rachel didn't want to refute Sandra's comment. Rachel had her own issues with God, but didn't want to get into that right now. So she simply smiled and excused herself to join her friends, who were already chatting and laughing around the table.

"Good morning, lovely ladies." Rachel pulled a large envelope out of her briefcase and dropped it on the table. "Meg Kierney, these are for you."

With a squeal, Meg pounced on the envelope, her pale blue eyes shining with anticipation. "Wedding pictures?"

"Fresh from the developer. Picked them up on my way here."

Anne and Pilar leaned over to look at the photos Meg had pulled out.

Old rivals Meg and Jared had met at the thirty-fifth anniversary for Tiny Blessings Adoption Agency. Meg had already gone through a bad divorce and Jared was a widower. When they discovered that their respective adopted boys, Luke and Chance, were twins separated at birth, the only practical solution was to get married for the sake of the boys. However, as they spent time together, they truly fell in love and later had another, private, more meaningful ceremony at the Chestnut Grove

Community Church. It was this ceremony that Rachel had pictures of.

"Oh. Look at Luke and Chance. They're so cute! I would love to have twins." Anne traced the faces of the boys with a longing look. "Actually, I would love to have kids, period."

"You will," Pilar said, reaching over and hugging their friend. "You just need to realize that you truly are beautiful. And someday some lucky man will see that, too."

When Rachel and her parents moved to Chestnut Grove, Pilar, Anne and Meg befriended Rachel, unfazed by her parents' wealth and unimpressed by her background. Rachel was a quick, bright student and as a result had skipped two grades, making her younger than the children she went to school with. Younger and, in spite of her brains, unable to defend herself in the rough and tumble that comes with changing schools. Her youth, combined with her New England accent and her parents' money had created a situation ripe for teasing from other girls who saw Rachel's quiet shyness as snobbery. One day some of the girls in her class had her cornered in the playground and were teasing her. Anne, Pilar and Meg had found her. The older girls had intervened and taken Rachel under their wing. Eight years ago, Rachel had moved away, but since her return she had slipped back into their lives as easily as if she had never been gone. Through the ups and downs of life, they had become her confidantes, advisers and dearest friends.

"Sorry I'm late. I had to meet with a couple of clients close to Winchester Park. I thought church would be longer." Rachel set her briefcase down on the floor beside her and brushed her hand over her hair. Still in place, surprisingly enough. When Eli Cavanaugh plowed into her, she was sure her hair had come loose.

"You look fine," Pilar said. Then she frowned, touching the smudges on Rachel's suit jacket. "Wait, what happened to you?"

"I interrupted a football game."

"What?"

Rachel waved one well-manicured hand. That little confidence was a mistake. "Never mind." She didn't want to talk about it. In fact, she preferred not to think about Eli, his shirt open, and his hair curling damply over his forehead.

"And you're blushing about that 'never mind,'" Pilar teased.

Meg glanced from Pilar to Rachel and laughed. "She is. Look at that, girls. I didn't think anything could faze our resident math whiz." She elbowed Rachel lightly. "C'mon. Who is he?"

"It's not a he." And her cheeks got even redder as she unconsciously brushed the other sleeve.

Pilar turned her around. "Look, a matched set on this arm. Someone has been manhandling our friend, amigas. Should we rush out to defend her honor or should we make her sit here and eat her fries without ketchup until she confesses who did it and why?"

"Unless, of course, she went through ketchup withdrawal and then we'd have to rush her to the hospital," Anne said.

"Too bad Dr. Cavanaugh is a pediatrician," Pilar said with a soft sigh, twirling her dark hair around her finger. "I bet Eli could melt this woman's cold heart with those dreamy green eyes…"

"Look at her. She turned red as a beet when you said Eli's name," Meg cried out.

They were getting dangerously close to the truth. Rachel knew her friends weren't going to quit until they solved her little mystery. "He was playing touch football and he ran into me while I was walking through the park, okay?" She looked around the group, from Anne's gentle expression to Meg's slightly cynical one to Pilar, who was grinning like she had discovered a deep, dark secret.

"I could run into that man any day," Anne said. "He's got an earthy appeal. He's almost as good-looking as…" She glanced around the group and laughed self-consciously. "As Jared," she said, flashing a smile Meg's way.

"Well, that's what happened," Rachel said with a dismissive wave of her hand. "Now, can we order? I'm starving."

"Eli's single, I heard," Meg said, looking from Anne to Pilar, still hot on the trail. "And isn't he Gracie's doctor?"

"Which has nothing to do with me," Rachel emphasized. So much for diversion. The conversation was getting out of hand.

"I don't know, Meg," Pilar said with a wink. "I think this girl has been struck by the arrow of love."

Rachel looked around at her so-called friends, sighed and pulled out the heavy ammunition. "He drives a motorcycle. Okay?"

The silence that followed this pronouncement showed Rachel how well her friends understood what that meant to her. She'd lost one man to a two-wheeled death machine.

"Are you ladies ready to order?" Miranda Jones stood in front of them, her arms clasped behind her back, her dark brown hair pulled up in a twist.

They were distracted in the flurry of ordering. After that, as they settled into their usual conversation, catching up on one another's lives, Rachel felt herself relax. They ribbed her about her dedication to her work. Pilar shared some of her struggles with one of her most recent cases, Meg talked about her twin boys, Anne about her work at the church. Rachel settled in to the conversation, thankful for her friends and their company.

Then, as she was halfway through her hamburger, her cell phone chirped.

"Leave it," Pilar, Meg and Anne all said at once.

But Rachel could no more let her cell phone ring than she could let her hair fly loose as her friends were always encouraging her to do.

She glanced at the call display. It was her father.

With an apologetic smile at her friends, she answered the phone, half turning away from her friends. "Hey, Dad."

"Rachel, honey—" His voice broke.

Concern flashed through Rachel. "Dad. What's the matter?"

"It's your mother. We're at the hospital. She broke her leg."

"I'll be there right away."

She closed her phone and pulled her wallet out. "That was my dad," she said, her voice trembling. "Sorry, girls, but I have to duck out. My mom broke her leg and is in the hospital." She laid some bills on the table, enough for her meal and a large tip.

"Oh, no. Do you want me to take you over there?" Anne asked, half rising from her seat.

"No, no." Rachel waved her down as she got up from the table. "I'll be okay. Really, I'll be fine."

"Let us know how she is," Pilar called out after her as Rachel hurried from the diner.

Fifteen minutes later she pulled open the door of the hospital and her brave words to her friends melted in the pervasive scent of disinfectant and ammonia. It rolled over her like a wave, dragging with it memories she wanted to be rid of.

Her steps faltered, but thoughts of her mother in pain drew her past her long-held dread of hospitals. The too-familiar nausea and fear gripped her with their icy fingers.

Stop. Stop! Your father needs you.

She pressed her fingertips to her forehead just as she heard her father's voice coming from one of the cubicles. She followed it, slipping past the curtain and stopping at the scene in front of her.

Gracie sat on the bed, and Eli, wearing a white lab coat over his shirt and blue jeans, was bent over her, shining a light in her eyes as her father held her still.

Her father looked up as she came in and gave her a wan smile.

"Where's Mom?" Rachel gave him a hug and glanced at Gracie, who twisted her head around to see who was here.

"Easy, Gracie." Eli's quiet voice drew the child's attention back to him, and she reached out for the stethoscope that hung around his neck as he finished his examination. "Let's have a look here."

"Mom's in surgery right now," her father said. "It was a bad break and they're not sure they can do what they need to here." He blew out a breath and wiped his shining forehead with a hanky.

"How did it happen?" Rachel struggled not to sway.

Don't faint. Not in front of the cowboy. Dad needs you.

"She was carrying Gracie down the stairs, lost her balance and twisted to break her fall. She caught her leg in one of the uprights on the staircase."

"How is Gracie?" Rachel studied the girl who, at first glance, seemed okay.

"So far so good. I don't see anything out of the ordinary." Eli snapped the light off and dropped it into a pocket of his lab coat. A light frown creased his forehead as his eyes took in Rachel. "You're a little pale."

"Rachel dislikes hospitals. She spent—"

"Do you know exactly what kind of break mom had?" Rachel felt rude interrupting her father like that, but Eli Cavanaugh didn't need to know her personal history.

"I'm sorry, I don't know," said Eli. "But I can go find out."

"Could you? Please?" Rachel gave him a careful smile and was surprised to see him return it. In spite of her surroundings, she felt it again, that little frisson of awareness. A sensation she hadn't experienced in a long time.

"I'll be right back." He touched Gracie on the nose and left.

The hiss of oxygen from a cubicle beside them, the rattle of carts and gurneys slipped into her consciousness, pulling memories along with them. She sucked in a breath, and another, fighting the light-headed feeling that threatened to overwhelm her.

Her father was wrong. She didn't dislike hospitals. She *despised* them. They held out the offer of hope, but really despair walked their halls. And now her mother was upstairs. How badly was she really hurt? What would happen to her?

"Here, honey. Sit down." Her father took her by the arm and sat her in the only chair in the curtained-off cubicle. "Eli was right. You look very pale."

Rachel shook off her growing panic. "I'm okay, Dad." Though, the way the room tilted around her gave lie to her protest.

After a few long slow breaths, she was standing up and in control again.

"Go down. Down," Gracie insisted, holding out her hands to her father.

"Can you take her, Rachel?" Charles asked, steadying Gracie, who was trying to wriggle off the bed.

Rachel was surprised to see her usually jovial father looking drawn. Then she glanced in the direction he was looking and saw Eli swishing the curtains aside, followed by another doctor. She hadn't heard either of them coming down the hall.

She glanced at Gracie, bit her lip and then, carefully, picked the child up off the bed, not sure if she was holding her right.

"I've got news. I'm afraid it isn't good," Eli said.

The serious tone of his voice quashed the faint wall Rachel had erected against her fear. He was bringing bad news. How could he?

"This is Dr. Mendoza. He can tell you more," Eli said.

In spite of Dr. Mendoza's smile, Rachel could see that he had his "professional" face intact, and her dread grew.

"We just got the results of your wife's X rays back." His almost black eyes took them both in, compassion in their depths. "She sustained a very serious fracture of the femur, complicated by what looks to be an older fracture farther up the bone. We want to talk about airlifting her to New York to be operated on there by an orthopedic specialist."

"New York?" Charles reached blindly behind him as if to steady himself.

Rachel, still holding Gracie with one hand, caught him and slowly pushed him toward the chair she had just vacated.

In the process Gracie overbalanced backward, her arms flailing. Rachel tried to grab her, but Eli was right there, catching the toddler just before she fell, settling her back in Rachel's arms.

"Thank you," Rachel said, feeling woefully inadequate. She couldn't even hold the child without almost dropping her.

"She does tend to be a bit restless," Eli said quietly, his hand still on Gracie's shoulders. "It's the C.P. that causes the sudden unexpected movements."

Rachel's stomach fluttered and, to her shame, she felt dizzy again.

"Can you please take her," Rachel asked, thrusting Gracie toward Eli before she fell, still holding the squirming child.

Eli gave her a questioning glance, but took Gracie, easily swinging her into his arms.

Rachel looked away, pulling in another long, slow breath as she moved past her father to lean against the bed before she turned back to Dr. Mendoza. "I'm sorry. You were telling us about my mother. What are her chances for a full recovery?"

He slipped his hands in the pockets of his lab coat, rocking lightly on his heels. "They are excellent. What slows it down is the intensive rehabilitation she will have to undergo. There's a facility connected to the hospital in upstate New York that specializes in orthopedics and will be taking care of her."

"When will she have to leave?" Rachel asked.

"We are setting up the transfer right now."

So soon, Rachel thought, still unable to process the fact that her always capable mother was disabled. But like a drowning swimmer, she clung to what the doctor told her. Doctors didn't use words like "excellent" unless there was a very good chance the patient would be all right.

"How long will she be there?" Charles asked.

"Approximately three to four weeks, which is contingent on how well she heals and how well the femur and surrounding tissue respond to therapy."

"That long." Charles slumped back, rubbing his chin with his hand, looking lost and forlorn.

He glanced up at Rachel, and she caught his hand in hers, her heart stuttering at the thought of her always strong and capable mother, helpless and in pain.

"I can't be apart from her that long," he said quietly.

"I know, Daddy." She squeezed his hand. "Is there a way he could go upstate and stay with her, Dr. Mendoza?"

"Of course. This institute gets people coming in from all over the United States. There are facilities where your father could stay. It would probably be better for your mother if he did."

"And what about Gracie?" Charles asked.

Dr. Mendoza looked over at Eli. "I think Dr. Cavanaugh can answer the rest of your questions. I must return to your wife and prepare her transfer." He shook Charles's hand, then Rachel's. "I'm sorry I don't have better news, but at the same time, we can be thankful that she didn't injure herself worse."

"Thank the good Lord, no," Charles agreed, but Rachel could hear his heart wasn't in the pronouncement.

"Can we take Gracie along?" Charles asked Eli as Dr. Mendoza left.

Eli shook his head. "I think it would be best if she stayed here." Eli glanced at Rachel, then back at Charles. "Beatrice is going to need your full attention if you want to help her, and it wouldn't be good for Gracie's health to get moved around that much."

Charles nodded, releasing Rachel's hand. He pressed his hands against his knees and, like an elderly man with too many worries pressing down on his shoulders, slowly got to his feet.

"Well, I guess I'll have to make a decision about our little girl." He passed his hand over his balding head and gave Rachel a careful smile.

"Rachel, honey. Would you be able to take care of Gracie?"

Chapter Four

"Me? Take care of Gracie?"

Rachel's shocked look was unmistakable to Eli. She pressed her hands together, then ran them down the sides of her skirt.

"But I've got so much to do…" She caught her lower lip between her perfectly straight teeth.

"She's attached to you, Rachel," Charles continued, the pain evident in his voice.

"I am not sure I could devote the time necessary to Gracie that she needs." Rachel pressed her lips together as if holding back words she knew condemned her.

Charles sighed lightly. "I would hire a nanny, but she doesn't take well to strangers. I know she is comfortable around you."

Rachel crossed her arms, as if weighing and planning this inconvenience in her life.

Just as Eli was about to make an alternative proposal, Rachel put her hand on her father's shoulder and straightened her shoulders. "However, she is my sister. I'll make sure she's taken care of."

"Thank you, dear," Charles said, patting his older daughter on the shoulder. He turned to Gracie and picked her up, holding her close. "Can I take her up to see Beatrice?" he asked Eli.

Eli held the curtain aside. "Beatrice might be too medicated to recognize her, but you can try."

Charles left first with Gracie, but as Rachel passed, Eli put a hand on her shoulder to stop her. She pulled back, her hazel eyes flashing her annoyance. Another small chink in her usually cool facade.

He held his hands up as if to show his innocence. "I'd like to talk to you for a moment," he said quietly.

Rachel glanced from him to her father, then nodded. "Sure. Just for a moment." She composed her features again. Businesslike. He suspected this was the face many of her clients and co-workers saw every day and for some reason he liked the annoyed look she had just given him much better. Made her seem more approachable.

Eli slipped his hands in the back pockets of his jeans and decided that being straightforward was the way to go with this woman. "If you can't take care of Gracie, I'm sure I could find an alternative for you."

Rachel's eyes narrowed. "I don't need an alternative. She's my sister. I can see to her care."

Her assured statement surprised him. He thought he was offering her a reasonable out. But it didn't sound like she wanted to take it.

"I've never taken care of a toddler before, but…" Her confident voice faltered for a moment. Then she lifted her chin and held his gaze as if underlining her next statement. "I will do this."

And for a moment, a grudging admiration snaked past

his concern. She was loyal, he gave her that. "I can give you what information you need if you are willing to come to my office," he said. "Can you bring Gracie by after this?"

Again a heartbeat of hesitation. "I can give you half an hour," she said.

Eli wondered what Rachel was going to do with Gracie after that. One thing was for sure. In spite of her insistence that she could take care of Gracie, he knew he would have to keep a close eye on the little girl. He wasn't going to let her care suffer for the sake of this Rachel woman's pride.

"I'll see you there in about twenty minutes."

She nodded, then swept past him, leaving in her wake a vague scent of peaches and almonds. But as she walked away, he wasn't surprised to see her pull out her Palm Pilot and then her cell phone.

He blew out a sigh as he caught sight of the clock in the outpatient department. Three o'clock. He had hoped to get some work done on his house today. He guessed that would have to wait.

He waved to the outpatient nurse as he strode out of the hospital. In minutes he was on his motorcycle and headed toward his office. As he rode he remembered Rachel's comment on his mode of transportation. Someday, he hoped to get a decent car. But for now the motorcycle was efficient and cheap. He didn't understand her reaction, but he wouldn't dwell on it.

Half an hour later Rachel sat across from his desk, a pen in one hand, notebook in the other. This woman was all business. "So what kind of care am I looking at for Gracie?"

"I have this basic information on Gracie's condition," he said, slipping a sheaf of papers across the table toward her. "Gracie has what is technically known as hemiplegia. In other words, her cerebral palsy affects one side of her body, her left arm and left leg." He explained the various people involved in her care—the physical therapist, the occupational therapist, and how often she had to see each. "She has been fighting an ear infection so she is on antibiotics." Eli picked up his pen and fiddled with it, avoiding Rachel's gaze. In spite of her insistence in the hospital, he could tell Rachel wasn't comfortable taking care of Gracie. If that was the case, how would she take this next bit of information?

"I get the feeling there's something else, Doctor," Rachel said with a note of impatience.

Of course she would be impatient. Probably had an urgent phone call to return. May as well lay it on the line.

"Gracie is afflicted with seizures from time to time. They have been coming more often and we are monitoring that carefully. So that means you need to keep track of them, as well. If she has too many and any severe ones, we will have to adjust her medication. Unfortunately, since she is fighting an infection, she's more susceptible to them right now."

Rachel glanced at the paper, then at Gracie, asleep in her stroller. He was surprised to see fear flash across Rachel's face. The woman was not as "in charge" as she liked to project.

"How do I know she's having a seizure and how bad are they?"

"They can vary. You need to look for tremors in her arms, flutters of her eyelids. If you have any major concerns, bring her in. I'm at the hospital three days a week, but I can come in at a moment's notice if it is serious enough. And if I can give you some advice…" Eli waited, realizing that Rachel would not appreciate what he had to say. But his first concern was for Gracie. Rachel needed to know what was at stake with this child.

"I've been taking care of Gracie since she was a newborn. I've said it before but it bears repeating, that while she looks good from a physical standpoint, she is still considered medically fragile. If we can keep her healthy for the next few years, then I know she can turn the corner. If not, we are looking at far more serious medical problems."

Rachel made a quick note, but Eli could see a faint tremble in her hand.

"What kind of medical problems are you talking about?"

"Fluid build-up in her brain that would necessitate a shunt. And with shunts come further infections and more problems." Okay, maybe he was laying it on a little thick, but she needed to know. The more information she had, the better decisions she could make.

And if he were to be perfectly honest, he was trying to goad her into reacting. Into being more than a cool, self-contained woman who saw Gracie as a duty. He wanted to know that she cared. That Gracie, who he had to admit was special to him, was going to be in good hands.

He handed her a card. "This is the hospital emergency number, my home number and my pager number. If you need me, call."

Rachel drew in a long, slow breath, as if absorbing the information with it. She slipped the paper in her briefcase and the card in her purse. "Okay. I'll see how this goes, then," she said, standing. Then, to his surprise, she reached across the desk to shake his hand. "Thanks for your time, Dr. Cavanaugh. I'm sure we'll be in touch."

He took her hand, surprised at how cool it felt.

Just like the rest of her, he thought.

She slipped her briefcase over her shoulder and Eli strode around the desk to open the door for her. But this time, as she passed him, she glanced up at him.

Their gazes met and held, and for a moment Eli felt it again. That tug, the age-old signal of two people attracted to one another in spite of circumstances.

He didn't know where it came from. She certainly had not encouraged it and he certainly wasn't looking. He was building up his practice, working on his house, paying off his loan, keeping his life ordered and on target.

He almost laughed as he watched her leave, putting down that flicker of awareness to the basic reality of his life. Though he casually dated, he knew he could not devote himself to a full-fledged relationship. And not with someone like Rachel Noble. Besides, he was devoted to his work.

Too devoted, according to his last serious girlfriend. She had other issues, he had found out, but she chose to make his job the main reason for the split. He found out afterward that her family had discouraged her from dating him mainly because they did not know what his background was. They did not know his biological parents, did not know what possibly sinister secrets lay in his genetics.

With a light laugh at the melancholy drift of his thoughts, he grabbed his helmet, left the office and headed for home.

The phone was ringing when he entered the house and a glance at call display made him smile.

"Hey, Mom, how are you?" he asked, tucking the phone between his shoulder and his ear as he bent over to pick up a shirt he had left lying on the floor. He knew his mother couldn't see the state of his house, yet he felt guilty.

"I'm just fine. Where were you all morning?" Peggy asked. "I tried a couple of times."

It wasn't hard to hear the expectant tone in her voice, which made Eli feel even more guilty.

"Ben and I had a Sunday morning football game and I got called to the hospital." He threw the shirt on a pile of laundry to be brought to the cleaners and slipped the DVDs he'd been watching the other night back in their cases.

"Ben was there, too?" He recognized the mixed message in her disappointed tone. It was as if she was saying that Eli's defection from church was difficult but not unexpected. That Ben, the apple of their eye, was heading down the same path seemed harder to take. Ben's reasons to stay away from church made perfect sense to Eli. Losing his beloved wife Olivia to cancer had pushed Ben away from God.

"It was his idea." As soon as he spoke the words, he felt like a heel. He was an adult. He didn't need to play these silly "he did it, too" games that he and Ben had grown up with.

It was just that his relationship with his adoptive parents always held undertones of his not fitting in. It hadn't helped that he had come to them as a child of six, after being orphaned by a car accident that took his only living relatives away from him. Ben, their other son, also adopted, had come as a newborn baby with no extra baggage. No mother, no father, no family that he knew of. The Cavanaughs had been able to start with a clean slate with Ben, whereas with Eli there was always a measure of friction. He had wanted to know about his parents but the Cavanaughs could tell him nothing.

Or *would* tell him nothing. Last year he had found a box of photos in the attic when he and Ben had helped their parents clean up. He had never seen them before: they were of him and his natural parents. Peggy and Tyrone had had them since he was young. When confronted with them, Peggy had said that the pictures had always made him very upset, so they put them away, then forgot about them. It seemed plausible; however, since then their relationship had become more awkward.

"You said you got called to the hospital," Peggy was saying. "I hope it wasn't anything too serious."

Eli thought of Rachel and Gracie and rubbed his forehead with his finger. "Not with my patient. She fell, but she's okay. How are you and Dad doing?"

"Good. But I was hoping we could come up sometime and help you and Ben finish the house."

"That's okay, Mom. I don't want you and dad to trouble yourselves. It's too far to travel from Florida to Richmond just to pound a few nails."

His mother's moment of silence created another twinge of guilt. "I see. Well, we will be up Labor Day. I hope we can see you then."

"Of course."

Peggy asked a few more general questions as the conversation drifted into the final goodbye.

Eli punched the button to end the call and tossed the

phone aside. Then he sat and leaned his head back against the soft leather of the couch as he looked around the house. Much as he did not want to admit it to his parents—or his brother Ben, for that matter—he'd been wondering more and more if buying this house wasn't a colossal mistake. All his life he had wanted a place of his own. A place that he could build up himself. It wasn't something he could easily explain to Peggy and Tyrone, much less to himself. Not even Ben understood why a confirmed bachelor wanted to tie himself down to a mortgage when he was still single.

But then, Ben did not have the memories of family that Eli had. And it was those vivid memories of a previous life that he clung to in the traumatic first year after witnessing his parents' lives snuffed out in front of him. He had loved his parents and it was that love that had caused some misunderstandings with Peggy and Tyrone Cavanaugh when he first went to live with them. It was as if they did not quite know what to do with a child who came with other memories.

So they never talked about his parents. Never mentioned them.

Eli had accepted that. Until he found the pictures.

He had taken the box of photos back with him, and now and again took them out as if trying to discover who these people were, these people who had given him life and had taken care of him those first few years.

Unconsciously he rubbed the scar on the back of his hand, a mute reminder of the accident.

He thought of Gracie Noble. She was young enough that she would not have any memories of her mother. As far as he was aware, the Nobles had encouraged contact with Gracie's mother, but the woman had left town as soon as she had put Gracie up for adoption.

Eli had been Gracie's doctor since she was born and it was really amazing that the child was as healthy as she was. Of course, she'd spent most of the first year of her life in and out of the hospital—whenever her mother seemed to think she needed a break from the demands of taking care of a handicapped child, which was every weekend and often during the week, as well. Eli had been the one to contact Pilar Estes, a social worker with Tiny Blessings—and a friend of Rachel's, he'd later discovered—with his concerns. Thanks to his intervention, Gracie had found a stable and loving home with the Nobles.

As Eli pushed himself up from the sofa, he thought of Rachel and wondered again if she was the best person to be taking care of Gracie. She had the same attitude Gracie's mother had had toward the child's handicaps. Though Rachel had tried to hide behind a cool facade, he had noticed the fear in her face when she first entered the hospital room.

He would have to see how she managed. If he had any doubts at all about Gracie's care, he would get her put into a better place.

"Reuben, I want you to leave Mrs. Binet to me," Rachel said, accelerating through a yellow light as she spoke on her hands-free cell phone. "If we push too hard, she could easily end up throwing it to some questionable organization. I'm going to be seeing her tonight and I want to advise her to wait." Provided Pilar could still baby-sit Gracie.

"We just need to find the right combination for her and I think I found one," said Reuben.

"Which one?" This was news to her. Last time she and Reuben had spoken to the woman, LaReese was still undecided.

"It's a new one that I'm investigating." He gave her the name, and Rachel frowned in puzzlement.

"Never heard of them."

"It is like a Make-A-Wish foundation and the focus is children of prisoners."

Rachel glanced at the clock on the dashboard of her car and stifled panic. She was already fifteen minutes late and the day care where she had brought Gracie this morning was another ten minutes away.

She slowed down, stuck behind a bus that was trying to make a left turn across two lanes of traffic. She glanced behind her and saw two lanes of traffic bumper to bumper behind her. This was not looking good. Today was the second day in a row she was going to be late.

"Doesn't sound like a match to me, Reuben," Rachel said, tapping her fingers restlessly on the steering wheel. "From our last meeting I got the impression that Mrs. Binet is looking more closely at health issues, rather than social ones."

"I think we could get her excited about this group. So far they seem on the up-and-up."

"The ink must barely be dry on their license. Why don't you give me what you've got? I'll see about showing it to her tonight."

"You don't trust me?"

Rachel glanced past the bus and saw a hole in the oncoming traffic she could slip through.

"It's not that I don't trust you…" The bus made the turn. Rachel accelerated through a yellow light, swerving around a car trying to make a last-ditch turn across her lane. She drew in a steadying breath. She was never this reckless. The sensible thing would be to pull over and finish the conversation. But time was her enemy.

"I feel personally responsible for seeing that Mrs. Binet is happy with our choice. If this works, she has more money earmarked for charitable donations."

"You put this on my desk, Rachel. Why are you micromanaging?"

Because that's how this Foundation got to where it did, she thought, stifling a sigh. People like Reuben thought that because her parents' wealth formed the backbone of the Foundation, money flowed easily in and out of the coffers.

Very few people, other than her closest assistants, realized how important relationships were in this business. Relationships, trust and a keen business sense. Money flowed out far more quickly than it flowed in.

When Rachel had taken over management of the Foundation, the books had not been anywhere near as healthy as they were now. Funds had been mismanaged and her parents, though good hearted and kind, had trusted the wrong people.

It had taken Rachel a few years and some hard decisions, but she had slowly brought the Foundation around. Now it enjoyed a healthy bank balance and had earned the trust of not only established and respected nonprofits who relied on them to organize fund-raisers, but also a vast number of wealthy patrons who trusted the Foundation to make good choices for them. However, in the past few months she had lost a few donors which made her nervous. She didn't want to have all her hard work fall away again.

"Reuben, I can't talk about this now. I still need to connect with Lorna and then pick up Gracie from day care."

Mrs. Binet was taking up far too much of her time, but she did not dare pass the woman on to Lorna or Reuben. LaReese Binet had specifically come to her, and the money they would be dealing with was enough to justify the personal hand-holding.

And somehow, in all of this, she had to figure out how to spend some so-called quality time with a little girl that still made her nervous. Is this what mothers did all the time? she wondered as she disconnected the phone. This juggling of time and need?

She took another corner, then realized she had turned too soon and desperately tried to find a place to turn around.

Fourteen minutes and thirty-five seconds later she pulled into the parking lot of the day-care center with a screech of tires. She grabbed her purse and keys and jumped out of the car, knocked her knee against the edge of the door and limped up the sidewalk of the day care, trying to ignore the ringing of the cell phone from her car.

She did not have time for this, she thought as she pulled open the glass doors of the day-care center. But her promise to her father and the faint challenge in Eli Cavanaugh's eyes kept her committed to Gracie's care. More importantly, Gracie was her sister. And no matter her discomfort, family takes care of family.

Gracie was waiting for her in the arms of the day-care worker, who looked pointedly at the clock. Her prim mouth and narrow eyes did not bode well for Rachel.

"We made our policy very clear when you enrolled your daughter in our program," the woman said.

"I understand…Mrs. Nelson," Rachel said, glancing at the woman's name tag. "And I want to apologize for picking up my *sister,*" she put extra emphasis on the word, "so late." She bent down and retrieved Gracie's diaper bag and then reached out for Gracie.

"We tried to contact you sooner." Mrs. Nelson looked down at Gracie and frowned. It was only then that Rachel noticed the girl's flushed cheeks and damp curls. "Gracie has not had a good day. The nurse took her temperature and it is elevated. She recommends that you take her to see her doctor as soon as possible."

"Like now?"

Her question made it sound like Gracie was just another chore shoe-horned between making a living and living. *Note to self,* Rachel thought as she took her sister in her arms, *think before you speak.*

"What I meant to say was, how urgent is this? Should I go immediately to the hospital, or should I monitor her situation?"

Mrs. Nelson lifted her shoulders in an exaggerated sigh as she gently brushed a curl away from Gracie's forehead. "I would suggest immediately. With Gracie's C.P., you need to be extra vigilant."

Which was why I brought her here and did not keep her at home.

"Then I'd better go." She could feel the heat of Gracie's body through her clothing. She did not dare look at her watch for fear of appearing even more insensitive. She was thankful that the hospital was not far from the day-care center.

Chapter Five

Twenty minutes later she pulled into the parking lot of the hospital, and as she hurried through the doors of the emergency room, the memories came rushing back.

She glanced down at Gracie, who lay slumped in her arms, and a new fear took over. As she strode to the intake desk, she wondered again how in the world she had thought she was capable of doing this.

For the past eight years she had battled feeling inadequate and out of control. Now she was holding a drooping child while answering the questions of a harried intake nurse juggling phone calls and questions from patients, nurses and doctors.

When she was done she walked back through the busy waiting room, fighting old and new fears, smelling the too-familiar odors peculiar to hospitals. She swallowed down a quiver of panic. She had to focus, for Gracie's sake.

Gracie whimpered in her arms, the heat from her body seeming to grow with each sweep of the minute hand over the clock. The nurses were busy with what nurses do, striding around looking capable and in charge. None of them glanced at Rachel.

Other people sat in the chairs, some bent over, others with dull, glazed looks on their faces. They were each caught up in their own misery and sorrow; they didn't care about Rachel and the toddler who seemed to be burning up in her arms.

Then Gracie stiffened, and panic clawed up Rachel's throat. If she believed that God would do anything, she would be praying by now.

But God hadn't paid attention to her before, and He wouldn't now.

She was relieved when Gracie relaxed again, moaning. She looked up at Rachel, her soft brown eyes holding a trust that Rachel felt she had broken. Rachel felt her heart skip in reaction. Then she looked away. Gracie was a duty. She could not afford to let this child wrap the tentacles of love and affection around her heart. Growing attached to a child like Gracie meant opening her heart to the potential of pain and loss.

And she wasn't going to do that to herself again.

After what seemed like hours, a nurse came and escorted her to a curtained-off cubicle. Rachel set Gracie on the gurney.

The nurse ran through a checklist of questions, allergies, medication. Rachel answered as best she could.

When she was done, the nurse inserted a thermometer into Gracie's ear just as a doctor came striding down the hallway toward them. His white coat flared out behind him as he flipped through a chart, a pen clamped between his lips, a stethoscope draped over his neck, reading as he walked. He looked capable. In charge.

It was Eli.

Rachel's heart skidded in relief.

He glanced sidelong at the intern who was keeping pace with him, talking. He stopped by the cubicle, nodding at what the intern was saying, made a few notes on the chart, then handed it back to the intern. As he did, he glanced around the room and his gaze caught Rachel's.

She felt the same tingle of reaction she had the first time their eyes met. She tried to dismiss it, to blame it on the feeling of deliverance she felt. The feeling that she was no longer alone with this sick child.

But woven through it she could feel the echoes of an older emotion. One she had convinced herself she would never let herself feel again.

One that she had felt a brief surge of when he had shaken her hand at her parents' place.

He walked to her side with an easy rolling gait as if there was no reason to hurry. Then he glanced at the nurse who was marking something on Gracie's chart.

"So what seems to be the problem?" he asked, glancing from Rachel to Gracie, then to the nurse.

"She's running a fever," Rachel said.

"I just took her temperature," the nurse said. "Slightly elevated, but nothing to be concerned about."

Rachel blinked, puzzled, then looked from Gracie's flushed face to Eli. "Slightly elevated? She felt so hot."

Eli glanced at the chart, then put his hand on the toddler's forehead. Gracie smiled up at him as if suddenly all was well in her world.

"Are you still giving her the antibiotics?"

"She has a couple of days to go."

"Well, they seem to be working. But just to be on the safe side, I'll check her more thoroughly."

Rachel hadn't noticed earlier how soothing his voice could be.

"How are you managing with her?" he asked.

"Well, it's only been a day and I'm already here, so that hardly says much for my capabilities," Rachel said. Gracie whimpered and reached out. Again she could not understand why the child seemed so attached to her. It was not as if Rachel had encouraged it. Gracie made her feel vulnerable. Taking care of her, even for a day, had intensified the feeling.

"You did the right thing. With kids like Gracie things can turn around quite quickly, either way," he said with a lazy smile that created a faint quiver in her midsection. She looked away.

"Did you take her temperature yourself before you came here?" Eli asked, looking in Gracie's ears, his fingers gently probing her neck.

"The lady at the day care center recommended I bring her in."

Eli listened to Gracie's heart, then put the stethoscope away. "You brought her to a day-care center? I thought you were taking care of her at your parents' place?"

His voice had taken on an edge that made Rachel stiffen. "No. I have a full-time job. I can't simply drop it to take care of Gracie."

Eli slipped his stethoscope into the pocket of his doctor's smock and asked the nurse beside him to leave. Then he turned to Rachel, his arms crossed over his chest. "There is no 'simply' about taking care of Gracie," he said. "A day-care center is not the best alternative for her. I would advise you to find something else."

The smile was gone, as was the warm tone of his voice. It shouldn't annoy her, but it did.

"It's not like I just dropped her off at the nearest one I could find," she said, feeling defensive. "I spent the first afternoon I had her researching day-care centers, and found one that is certified to take care of children with special needs. And right now, all I need is for you to tell me what's wrong with her."

Eli sighed lightly but turned back to the toddler, who was reaching for Rachel, her eyes tearing up. Her lower lip glistened and she looked as if she was going to cry again. Rachel stroked her back, waiting.

"She's fine. Yes, her temperature is slightly elevated, but that could just as easily be because she is upset. Her one ear seems a bit red, but that will go down with the antibiotics. If she starts to fuss, give her some children's Tylenol and monitor her temperature. I'll give you a list of things you might want to have on hand," he said, scribbling notes on a piece of paper. He ripped the paper off the pad and held it out to her.

Rachel felt suddenly foolish, yet relieved to know that Gracie was basically okay. "Thanks for the advice," she said, putting the paper into her purse.

"I'd like to see her day after tomorrow to make sure that we are staying on top of this infection. Is there any time that works best for you?"

Midnight, she thought. It was usually about that time that she managed to go to bed. Counting the Sunday of her mother's accident, Rachel had had Gracie only two days, but already her life had gone from busy to barely controlled chaos.

"Why don't you set up an appointment and I'll work it

into my schedule?" she said with a quick smile that did not seem to charm him one iota.

Not that she cared. As she had told her friends, Gracie's attractive doctor was not her type. As if she even had time for a "type." These days she felt as if she was juggling eight balls and if she let go of just one, all the rest would tumble to the ground. Her work was her life. If it fell, what would she have?

"Where can I reach you if I can't get you at home?"

She provided her work number and cell phone number. "Just leave a message with Lorna if you can't reach me at work. And my cell phone has an answering system. You have my parents' number. They have an answering system, too."

Eli gave her a wry smile. "All these numbers and I still might have to leave a message?"

"It's not difficult. I do it all the time."

She hadn't meant to sound so snippy, but something about him was still making her feel defensive. She picked Gracie up and the child wound her arms around Rachel's neck. In spite of her resolve, Rachel felt herself softening. Then she glanced at the clock and the feeling hardened into frustration. She was supposed to be meeting with LaReese in half an hour and now she had supplies to buy and a child to feed instead. She would have to reschedule and hope LaReese understood.

"I have to go," she said. "Thanks for seeing Gracie. I'll see you in a couple of days." And without a backward glance she left the emergency ward.

"I got a few ins on some potential nannies," Pilar said, dropping onto Rachel's couch holding the phone in one hand, a paper with a list of names in the other. "One of them used to be a nurse. A couple of them have some kind of medical training."

"You are a lifesaver," Rachel said to Pilar, slipping papers into her briefcase. "If I can get a nanny, I won't have to worry about packing her around, as Eli so delicately put it. For now, I'm glad you could come and watch Gracie for me. Are you sure you're going to be okay with her?"

"Hey. The doctor said she was fine, and I'm a super friend."

"If you can find a capable nanny, you will not only be a super friend, you'll be a lifesaver."

"So I'm round and holey?" Pilar smiled, then leaned back in the low couch and twirled a long strand of dark hair around her finger. "But friends, even super friends, are also honest, and honestly girl, you look frazzled, which is not the capable Rachel we know and love."

"I'm tired. Too many things on my mind," Rachel said, sorting through the papers she needed to take to LaReese's place. "I'm going flat out at the Foundation and LaReese is being difficult to deal with and I can't afford not to mollycoddle her. I've lost a couple of donors in the past couple of weeks and one of our charities wants us to do their golf tournament."

"Why don't you get Lorna to do it?"

Rachel paused for a moment, considering it, then shook her head. "I can hardly dump this on her shoulders."

"So you dump it on yours."

"My shoulders are more experienced than hers," Rachel said absently, riffling through the papers she had laid out.

"It wouldn't kill you to pass a few things on, my friend

the micromanager. I would love to see you have some kind of life beyond the Foundation."

Rachel gave her a smile. "My life *is* the Foundation. I don't need more."

"Everyone needs more," Pilar said softly. "I enjoy my job, but it isn't everything for me. I'm still looking for love."

"My friend the romantic." Rachel slipped the rest of the papers in her briefcase. "Life is a whole lot easier if you keep things, well, simple."

"Taking care of Gracie and working six days a week is hardly simple."

"It will be if you find me a capable nanny. Then I won't have to cart her around so much. Eli was right about that." Though, it hurt to admit it.

"I'm still surprised you agreed to take care of her."

"What else could I do? Though, I have to confess she still makes me nervous."

"Why is that?"

Rachel stopped and bit her lip. Though Pilar, Meg and Anne had known her for many years, none of them fully understood the pain that she had buried deep. She didn't always understand it herself. She only knew that Gracie's vulnerability, the fact that she needed Rachel, had slowly pried those feelings to the surface once again.

"Is this about Keith?" Pilar asked.

Rachel looked into her friend's eyes and for a moment confusion slipped past her usual self-control. "It was a huge loss."

"But that shouldn't keep you from caring about someone again. I don't think God meant for you to be alone the rest of your life."

"Then why did He take Keith from me?" She heard a

cry from Gracie's room and stiffened. "And why did he make that little girl the way she is?"

Pilar sighed heavily, her arms crossed over her chest in a defensive gesture. "You are more intelligent than that, Rachel."

Rachel held her hand up. "I'm sorry. I know all about sin and evil and that God uses everything, so don't start with the mini-sermon."

"You know it, you just don't want to believe it." Pilar touched her friend on the shoulder. "And even more than that, I think you don't dare open your heart again because you don't believe God uses everything for our good. Yes, there is pain in relationships, but that is all part of the chance we take when we open our hearts."

"Well, right now I don't have time for heart stuff. I haven't met anyone who is my type." She pulled out a mirror and gave her makeup and hair a quick going-over.

"Not even Eli Cavanaugh?"

Rachel tried to ignore the little rush she felt at the mention of his name.

"I think he's very attractive," Pilar continued. "He's got this strong gentleness thing happening. Very appealing. And by the flush I can see creeping up your neck, I think you are thinking the same thing."

Rachel slipped the strap of her briefcase over her shoulder and grabbed her purse, trying to ignore her friend's teasing. "He is attractive," she conceded, knowing that if she didn't, Pilar would harp on her until she did. "But right now I don't have time for anyone, appealing or not."

"Have a good time, hon," Pilar called out as Rachel walked to the door. "If Eli calls, I'll tell him you said hello."

Rachel just tossed a wave over her shoulder and left.

* * *

"We're supposed to maintain our sanity in this noise?" Pilar handed Kelly Young the file she had been working on and glanced back over her shoulder. "I'm just thankful it's quitting time."

Kelly frowned as the screech of nails being yanked out of the wall in the far end of the building competed with their conversation. She brushed a hand over her streaked blonde hair, as if checking for dust. As director of Tiny Blessings Adoption Agency, she liked to maintain a professional appearance.

"I just asked Ben to pull off the damp drywall. He promised me the worst of this would be finished by the time we get back to work."

Though the adoption agency had been fully restored some years ago, in the past few days the heating system had been giving them problems. Over the weekend one of the radiators had sprung a leak and soaked into the drywall of an older, empty room. They had been using the room for storage of odds and ends and Kelly had hoped to turn it into a proper meeting room.

She had phoned a plumber who had managed to fix the system and now Ben Cavanaugh, a local carpenter, was taking the old drywall down.

Though she had a pressing appointment in twenty minutes, the working day was almost over. Hopefully Ben would be done the worst of it before they all returned to work the next day.

"Did Ann get the criminal record check on this family?" Kelly asked, flipping through the file Pilar had just given her.

"She was waiting to get it faxed to her."

"What do you think of this match?" Kelly asked.

"Professionally I think it's a very good match. Personally, I think it will be fantastic." As a social worker for Tiny Blessings Pilar was directly involved in matching prospective families to children being put up for adoption.

Pilar helped herself to a chocolate from a box that was part of a thank you basket that had been sent to Kelly from a grateful family who had adopted a child through their agency.

Kelly glanced up at Pilar and felt a flicker of envy. Somehow, in spite of eating what she wanted, Pilar managed to maintain her slim figure. With her straight black hair and black eyes, she was stunning and Kelly was surprised that she was still single.

"So I guess now all we need to do is…" Kelly stopped as Ben, the carpenter, put his head into the doorway.

"I found something you might want to have a look at," he said to Kelly.

Frowning, Kelly got up, followed by Pilar.

They passed Ann, Kelly's secretary on the way out. She looked up at them as they followed Ben.

"What's going on?" she asked.

Kelly paused at Ann's desk, laying the file on it. "I don't know. Ben wants to show me something in the room he's working on."

Curious, Ann got up and followed them as well.

When they got to the room, Ben was standing by the studs he had just exposed. But instead of an orderly row of two by fours, in the middle of the wall, was what looked like a doorway and beyond that, Kelly saw a small room instead of an exterior wall.

"What is it?" Kelly asked.

"This is a false wall built later," Ben said. "I think this is the doorway."

Kelly walked over to the opening and caught the scent of moldering paper and damp cardboard from the room.

"Here. I'll shed a little light on the subject," Ben said pulling out a flashlight and shining it into the room. "Let me go in first. I want to make sure it's okay."

Kelly glanced over her shoulder at Pilar and Ann who looked as puzzled and as curious as she was.

"There's a whole bunch of boxes in here," Ben's muffled voice called out. "But it looks to be okay."

Kelly followed him in and stopped dead, her eyes following the beam of light that Ben shone over the contents of the room. The room was only about four feet deep. Barely large enough to hold the two of them, but alone each end were stacked boxes.

"Take one out into the other room so we can look at it better," Kelly asked Ben, now completely baffled. What was in these boxes and why were they hidden away in a secret room like this?

Once the box was in the outer room, Ben pulled the flaps open.

It was full of files.

Pilar and Ann came closer as Kelly knelt down and pulled one out. She didn't recognize the name written along the tab.

"Does this look familiar?" she asked Ann and Pilar.

Ann took the file from Kelly's hand and flipped through it. Then frowned. "The names look familiar, but I'm sure we have a copy of this file in our main filing system," she said. "I wonder why there would be a second copy."

"Take it to your desk. We can look at it better there," Pilar suggested.

Kelly glanced at her watch. She was going to be late. "I'd like to go over it together. It will have to wait for now."

She brushed her skirt off and smoothed her hand over her hair hoping she looked presentable. Her makeup she could check on the way.

"Here, I'll take that," Ben said, easily picking up the box. "Where do you want it?"

"Put it in my office," Kelly said. She bit her lip as she looked at the hole in the wall. "Do you mind to waiting to finish this until we can have a better look at those other boxes?" she asked Ben.

He shrugged. "I don't mind quitting early."

Kelly got up, a feeling of unease slipping through her. The previous director of the agency, Barnaby Harcourt, ran things his own way but was very suspicious even by Barnaby's standards.

She looked at Pilar, Ann and Ben. "I don't know what's in the files, but for now, we better keep this between us. It could be nothing, but I'm guessing that those files were hidden for a reason."

They all nodded and as they left, Kelly locked the room.

Ben brought the box to Kelly's office just as Florence, the cleaning lady came in the front door.

She frowned and glanced at the clock on the wall, as if questioning what they were doing here so late.

Kelly shot a warning glance at Pilar, Ben and Ann. "I'm sorry Florence, but something important came up." She took a moment to compose herself, trying to find the right way to put off Florence being around without arousing suspicion. "Ben didn't get finished here like I had hoped he would so it's rather pointless to have you clean up today."

Florence shot Kelly an annoyed look. "But I get paid to do this. I can't come for a couple of days."

Kelly made a snap decision. "You still get paid for your

time today. It's just rather pointless to clean up when Ben is still working."

Florence looked from Kelly to Ann to Pilar with narrowed eyes. "Okay. But I don't like this. I had to come out special to do this job."

Kelly bit back a frustrated sigh. One of these days she was going to find a replacement for this contrary woman. "I'm sorry, Florence. I was hoping Ben would be finished by now."

"I'm a little slow is all," Ben said, flashing a smile at Florence.

She was momentarily mollified. Then without another word, she turned and left.

"I've got to run," Kelly said, looking at the others. "But please, don't say anything to anyone about this."

"Of course not," Pilar said.

"Good. Then we'll see you tomorrow," Kelly said.

But as she hurried off to her next appointment, she wondered again what was in those files and why they had been hidden.

"I'm sure it's a very good charity, but we haven't done a background check on it," Rachel said, keeping her smile in place.

"Reuben seemed quite excited about it." LaReese fingered a swath of platinum-blond hair behind her ear. "And truthfully, I haven't found anything that you have brought me that matches his excitement."

Rachel didn't like the idea that Reuben was winging it on his own.

"What matters more is that *you* are excited about the charity," Rachel said quietly. "And to tell you the truth, right now we know very little about this one. Your money is yours to do with as you please, but I am sure that you want to know that it is being handled wisely, as well."

"Reuben wanted to bring this charity under the Foundation's umbrella," LaReese added. "You could keep an eye on it then."

"Could you do one thing for me?" Rachel asked, leaning forward. "Could you wait until we can do some proper background checks and I'm satisfied it is a good match for you?"

LaReese sighed, fingering the sapphire necklace that hung in the hollow of her throat. "I could, though I would like to get involved with something as soon as possible." She gave Rachel a surprisingly vulnerable smile. "Dale entrusted me with this money, and the sooner I do it the sooner I can feel I fulfilled his dying wishes."

"I understand," Rachel said. "But the best way to keep faith is to give it to a charity that will use his money in the most stewardly way."

LaReese gave her a smile. "You sound like your father," she said. "He has always been an example of God's love working in everyday life."

Rachel felt a twist of bittersweet pain. She had not spent much time with God in the past few years. LaReese's words brought her back to a time when she prayed more, read her Bible more. When Church and faith were as much a part of her as breathing.

She wondered what it would take for her to recover her faith and trust in God. And if she really wanted it back.

She smiled at LaReese and glanced discreetly at her watch. It was time to leave.

"Like I said, please give us a little more time to do this right," Rachel said, as LaReese escorted her down the wide stairs to the massive front door of her mansion. "Your husband would not want you to rush on this, I am sure."

But LaReese's vague nod did not inspire much confidence.

Later a very frustrated and tired Rachel parked her car in the underground parking lot and resisted the urge to bang her head against the steering wheel. She had used two hours of rare and valuable time on LaReese but still had nothing to show for it.

Pushing down a sigh, she walked through the parking garage, her steps echoing in the half dark. She hit the button for the elevator and got in. It stopped at the main floor. The doors swept open.

And Eli Cavanaugh stepped inside.

He was casually dressed, wearing a leather jacket. His motorcycle helmet was tucked under his arm.

"Hi. What are you doing here?" she asked, her breath caught somewhere between her throat and her chest as she took a step back, disliking the school-girl crush feeling he had created in her.

She blamed her defensiveness on Pilar and her heavy hints a few hours previous.

His slow-release smile did nothing to ease that breathless feeling. "Just thought I would stop by and see how you are making out with Gracie." He frowned as he noticed her briefcase. "Were you out?"

"Yes, I had an important meeting." She felt impolite and suddenly a bit foolish. Though she could just as easily have stayed home for all the good it had done.

"As are all your meetings," he said, his smile turning into something less welcoming.

She felt her spine stiffen at the faint note of condemnation in his voice. "My friend is a very capable babysitter," she said, lifting her chin in the air.

"I'm sure she is." He stood back when the elevator stopped.

As Rachel stepped onto her floor, she heard the muffled sound of a child crying. It came from her condo.

She opened the door in time to see Pilar carrying a screaming Gracie across the room, the child's arms pushing at Pilar's chest.

Rachel dropped her briefcase and ran to her friend's side. Gracie saw Rachel and swung around in Pilar's arms, reaching out to her. Tears flowed down her flushed cheeks and her curls were damp with sweat.

"It's okay, baby," Rachel said, taking her in her arms, stroking her back. Guilt swept through her as she felt how warm Gracie was. "What's wrong with her?"

"She woke up crying half an hour ago. I gave her some medication, but it doesn't seem to be working."

Then Gracie slumped against her and Rachel panicked. "What is she doing? Is she okay? I can't see her."

Eli had his hand on Gracie's back, steadying her. He touched the toddler's temple, suddenly all business. "How much did you give her?" he asked Pilar.

She told him and he nodded, his hand covering the child's head. "We need to take her temperature."

"I've got an electronic thermometer," Rachel said, leading the way to the bathroom.

Behind them a cell phone trilled, and Rachel and Eli glanced back. Pilar held her phone up with an apologetic look.

Eli inserted the thermometer into Gracie's ear. When he

checked it, he bit his lip. "The medication should have kicked in by now. We need to cool her down quickly. If we don't, she might have a seizure." Eli knelt down by the bathtub. "I'll run the water, you undress her." He turned on the taps, stripped off his coat and held his hand under the water to check the temperature.

Rachel cleared off a small bench beside the bathtub and sat down. She pulled Gracie's unresisting arms from her sleeper, peeled her diaper off. It was still dry. She was burning up, and Rachel wondered how such a small body could generate so much heat.

Rachel slipped her own blazer off and heedlessly let it fall to the tiled bathroom floor. She tried to roll her sleeves up, but couldn't manage.

Eli looked over his shoulder and saw her dilemma. Kneeling down in front of her, he unbuttoned the cuffs of her silk blouse and gently rolled the sleeves up. It was a strangely tender gesture, and Rachel felt a quiver in her midsection as his fingers brushed her arms.

"Okay, very slowly lower her into the water," Eli said.

Rachel knelt beside him and did as he told her. As soon as Gracie's body touched the water, she sucked in a quick breath and then started to scream in earnest, bucking stiffly in Rachel's arms.

"It's too cold," Rachel said, pulling her back again. "She feels like she's having a seizure."

"She's just having a temper tantrum." Eli caught Rachel's arm and stopped her. "It feels cold to her because she's so hot."

Rachel turned her head and met his eyes. His smile made tiny crinkles at the corners of his eyes and showed the hint of a dimple in one cheek. "She'll be okay. Trust me," he said quietly.

And to her surprise, Rachel did.

Gracie screamed again, but this time Rachel felt more relaxed. Eli had said it was okay. So then it was.

Gracie shivered and flailed in the water, but Rachel kept her there.

"Dribble a bit of water on her forehead," Eli said, still crouched beside her. "Not too much or it will be too much of a shock."

"Are you going to need me any more?" Pilar asked, standing in the doorway of the bathroom, cell phone in hand. "I just got an emergency call I can't pass on."

Rachel shook her head and turned her attention back to Gracie. "I think we'll be okay." She glanced at Eli who knelt beside her. "Won't we?"

"We will," he said quietly.

"You sure?" Pilar asked.

"I'm sure," Rachel said with conviction.

"Okay. I'm out of here." Pilar left, and suddenly Rachel and Eli were alone.

By the time they were done, Gracie was shivering and her lips were changing from bright red to pale pink. Rachel pulled her dripping body out of the bathtub and wrapped her in the large fluffy towel Eli had pulled off the towel rack.

"Do you have some children's Tylenol?" he asked, pushing himself to his feet and wiping his own hands.

"I bought a bunch of stuff shortly after I saw you," Rachel said, rubbing the now shivering little girl dry. "It's on the counter behind you."

"I'm surprised she spiked a temp," Eli said as he pulled

out the bottle. "She was fine when I saw her this afternoon."

"And when I left this evening." Rachel finished drying Gracie off and bent over to pick up the sleeper she had discarded on the floor.

Eli reached for it at the same time, and for a moment their fingers brushed. Rachel kept her grip on the sleeper and her emotions this time. She blamed her earlier reaction to him on her fear for Gracie.

But as she got up to bring Gracie to the bedroom, she couldn't stop herself from glancing at Eli, surprised to find him looking at her. He held out the bottle of Tylenol.

"Just give her the recommended dosage," he said as she took the bottle.

She nodded, and this time she left without looking back.

By the time she got Gracie changed, medicated and settled into bed, she felt a little more in control. Gracie lay down this time without a fuss, and Rachel stood beside her crib, waiting for her to settle down. Her thick lashes fluttered a moment, and Rachel saw her eyes go glassy. Then the child blinked and her eyelids slowly drooped shut. Rachel waited a moment, just to make sure.

The light from the hallway darkened, and she glanced over her shoulder to see Eli silhouetted in doorway, looking for all the world like a concerned father.

"How is she doing?" he whispered.

"I think she's asleep." Rachel waited another moment, just to make sure. Then she tiptoed out of the room and closed the door.

"You might want to leave it open just a crack," Eli said quietly. "She's used to light during the night."

Rachel frowned her puzzlement at him. "How do you know?"

"She spent a lot of time in the hospital."

"Gracie was that ill as a baby?"

Eli's laugh was without humor. "Whenever her mother wanted to get rid of her for the weekend, she'd manufacture some excuse to bring her to the hospital."

Fragments of conversation Rachel remembered fell into place. "My parents never said a lot about Gracie's mother."

"They never met her. By the time the hospital social worker was aware of the case, Gracie had been in the hospital for a while, waiting for her mother to pick her up. She never came." Eli slipped on his jacket and retrieved his helmet from the floor where he had dropped it moments before.

Rachel felt a sudden surge of compassion for the child now laying in her crib. "No wonder she gets so upset when people leave her."

"And that could be why she spiked the temperature."

They were standing by the front door now, their voices echoing in the wide expanse of Rachel's loft condo.

"I'm glad you were around to help."

"I'm sure Pilar would have known what to do. She's a very capable person." Eli turned the helmet over in his hands, his mouth curved up in a lazy smile.

And why should that innocuous commendation of her friend cause a nip of jealousy?

"She's also a good friend. I can't think of too many people who would be willing to baby-sit at a moment's notice."

"You are lucky in your friends."

Rachel just smiled, not sure what to say next. Chit-chat

with men was something she realized she was woefully out of practice at. Not a good indicator of her social life, she realized.

Eli didn't seem in a hurry to leave as he looked around her condo. "Nice place you got here," he said.

Rachel followed his gaze. "It's a bit big for me, but I like it."

Lights from downtown Chestnut Grove sparkled back through the floor-to-ceiling windows, adding to the warm glow of the sconce lights embedded in the rough-hewn walls.

"It is nice," he agreed.

The conversation was obviously winding down to either a goodbye or an invitation for coffee. Rachel bit her lip, wondering if she should ask him to stay awhile. It had been a long, long time since she'd had male company. When she moved to New York after Keith's death she had tried dating, but every man had fallen short of her ideal.

Even now, though the memories of him had faded, the potential of pain was like a hidden bruise in her life. Only painful when touched.

She did not want to open herself to that again.

"Thanks for stopping by," she said quietly, making the wisest choice. Eli was Gracie's doctor. He should never be anything more.

He tossed his motorcycle helmet from one hand to the other and Rachel's resolve to steer clear of him hardened.

"Well, if anything changes, let me know." He tossed her another smile, then left.

As the door clicked closed behind her, Rachel took a deep breath to slow her heart down. She had made the best decision. Her life was too complicated and too busy right now for anything else.

So why did she feel suddenly so very alone? Why did her once funky and inviting condo now seem so large and empty?

She pushed the melancholy feelings aside and walked back to Gracie's room to check on her one more time before she settled into her office to catch up on some work.

Chapter Six

When the alarm clock went off the next morning Rachel dragged herself out of confused dreams. Then she heard Gracie fussing, and any remnants of sleep that still clung to her fuzzy mind were dashed away.

She stumbled out of bed and down the hallway to Gracie's crib. It was a secondhand unit she had borrowed from Meg.

Gracie sat in the corner, crying, but seemed okay. She settled a bit when Rachel pulled her out. However, as Rachel worked through an entirely unfamiliar routine of feeding and washing and changing a toddler, Gracie was fractious, alternately clinging to Rachel, then pushing her away and looking around the condo as if trying to find something familiar aside from her older sister.

Every time Rachel tried to put her down, she cried, which made getting ready for work challenging. Finally Rachel simply had no choice but to ignore her and get her hair done and makeup on with the noise of her cries piercing her ears.

Rachel was grateful when the nanny promised by Pilar arrived half an hour early. She was an older woman, very efficient. Very capable. Even her name instilled a feeling of confidence, Frances Simpson.

As Rachel showed her around the condo, though, she saw it through the caregiver's eyes. It was a great place to live, but somehow the high ceilings and large open living spaces that had created the appeal Rachel was paying for, now seemed cold and sterile. Not like a home at all.

The nanny was all diplomacy and tact, and Rachel hoped Pilar had explained the circumstances to her—because as she put on her suit coat and picked up her briefcase, she suddenly felt like a neglectful mother.

Which was emphasized when Gracie started crying again.

Had Gracie screamed and carried on, Rachel might have had an easier time leaving. But the child only looked at her with a woebegone expression as fat tears slid silently down her cheeks. Her quiet misery plucked at Rachel's heart and made her think of Gracie being left behind in the hospital while her mother headed out.

She couldn't get the picture out of her head as she drove to work, as she waded through the many messages that had piled up in the hour she had been waylaid while she got Gracie settled in.

Shortly after she got to the office she had the phone tucked under her ear as she scribbled her name on a couple of letters that Lorna had put in front of her. She covered the phone with one hand as she looked up at the woman.

"Lorna, can you get Daniel from the fund-raising division to come up here? I've got a few questions on the last statement he gave me."

"I'll get him right away. Oh, and Reuben dropped off the information on that charity for Mrs. Binet. Reuben asked me to set up a meeting with her here for Monday next week."

Rachel frowned. "I usually meet LaReese at her home."

"I know, but Reuben told me to make the meeting here."

"May I remind you that I'm in charge here, not Reuben."

Lorna fiddled nervously with the papers she held. "I'm sorry if I made a mistake. It was just that Reuben insisted, and I didn't dare…"

Rachel held her hand up in a soothing motion. "Don't worry. Reuben can come on strong. I'll take care of him. In the meantime, I want you to cancel the meeting. La-Reese is very uncomfortable going out into public places." A fact which had made dealing with her doubly difficult. "What I do want you to do is set up a meeting with the chairman of that new group, the one for autistic children. The early intervention group." Rachel tapped her pen on the desk as she tried to dredge the name out of her mind. Usually the information was right there. But she was feeling punchy this morning and out of sorts. As she worked she could not get the picture of Gracie out of her mind.

"I know which one you mean. I'll set it up right away."

As Lorna left, Rachel wondered if she shouldn't do as her friends had always suggested. Let her assistants do more of the work. That was why they were called *assist*-ants.

Though they were both willing, she was also sensing a growing tension between the two. Lorna had been dropping vague comments about Reuben for the past few weeks and Reuben's behavior lately did not instill much confidence. If Reuben was giving Lorna conflicting information, this created one more situation Rachel had no time to deal with.

The rest of the morning slipped by, and at noon, she phoned Frances Simpson and was relieved to hear that so far, things were going well. Gracie wasn't running a temperature and she was just about to be put down for a nap.

Rachel hung up the phone but could not stifle the niggling doubts she had. She glanced at her calendar for the rest of the day.

She had to show up at the opening of a group home the Foundation had helped set up. After that, some research into an organization that had applied to Noble, then numerous phone calls about the annual Noble Foundation Picnic that was held at her parents' estate. She pinched the bridge of her nose, wondering if she could find a few moments to sneak away and see Gracie.

The ringing of the phone pulled her back to her work. "Hey, Anita, how are you?" she asked, recognizing the caller as her former secretary.

"Bored." Anita sighed. "How is the Foundation doing?"

"Not too bad." Rachel didn't want to give her any more particulars than that. She knew that losing some of their donors was not her own fault, but she still felt it reflected on her. "So what can I do for you?"

"I just wanted to see if you would be willing to let me use you as a reference. I'm looking for another job."

"You've only been working at this job for a couple of months."

"I know. It makes me sound irresponsible."

"Hardly. You were here before I came." In fact, Rachel often wondered if Anita hadn't quit *because* of Rachel. "So what's the problem with the new place?"

"Same as the previous. Not enough responsibility." Anita stopped, then sighed lightly. "I'm sorry, Rachel, that slipped out."

"It's okay," Rachel said. But she knew it wasn't. When Rachel had first come to the Foundation, things were run so haphazardly that she had to personally oversee many of the operations just to get them on track. She knew what she wanted and had a hard time translating that to other people, Anita included. Now she had two assistants, but was still having difficulty letting go. "But I would gladly give you a reference."

"Anybody home?" Reuben put his head through the doorway.

Rachel motioned for him to come in. "I should go, Anita. Thanks for calling and good luck in your new job." She rang off and sat back into her chair. "What have you got for me?"

"I haven't been able to find out a lot. What I'd really like is to head down there and talk to the people face to face. I could drive down over the weekend and be back by Monday."

Rachel bit her lip, trying to think of all the work she needed to get done in the next few days. She could put a few things off that Reuben could take care of when he came back.

"I am not a hundred percent convinced this is the group for her, nor do I have a lot of time for this personal hand-holding she insists on."

"Let me take care of her when I come back," he said, grinning. "I know how to do this."

Rachel turned her chair slightly as she looked at him. "If you know, why did you get Lorna to set up an appointment with her in this office?"

"What?" Reuben looked genuinely puzzled, then angry. "I didn't ask Lorna to do that for me."

Rachel just stared at him. As he held her gaze, she could not help but think of what Lorna had told her a few days ago. How uncomfortable she felt around Reuben. How pushy he was.

His go-to nature was one of the reasons she had hired him, but she wondered if these very same qualities weren't becoming a detriment.

"Rachel, I didn't ask Lorna to set up a meeting," Reuben continued, resting his hands on her desk and leaning toward her. "And if she says I did, well, she's lying. And truthfully I think you need to check on a few other things she's doing."

His combative words did nothing to reassure her. "Lorna does a good job," she said.

"Could be. But I think she's doing a few other things, as well, besides lying about what I've asked her to do."

Rachel sighed quietly. Hiring two assistants had seemed like a good idea; now she was not so sure. Each had strengths, but in the past few weeks, she had sensed a tension between the two that only seemed to be escalating.

"Setting up the meeting must have been some kind of mix-up on Lorna's part. Don't worry, I got her to cancel it."

"That's good. I know LaReese doesn't like going out. She told me as much the last time I saw her."

Rachel frowned. "When did you see her?"

Reuben straightened and shifted away from her. Retreating. "She called me last week. Asked if I could stop by. She had a few questions about the Foundation."

"Considering that I've been working for the Foundation longer than you, this surprises me."

Reuben spread his hands out in a "what could I do?" gesture. He flashed his most charming grin. "Maybe she likes me."

"I'm sure she does." Rachel smiled back, but it wasn't sincere. "In the future I would prefer you run any contact with her past me first, okay?"

"Sure. I'm sorry. I just thought because we had been there together the last time…" He let the sentence hang.

"Anyway, go and check out that charity. If she's interested in it and it's legitimate, then we should be okay. And I'm glad we got this straightened out." Except, Rachel didn't feel like she had. She now had to talk to Lorna to find out what *she* knew.

The next few hours slipped by without further complications. But just as she was about to call it a day, she got a frantic phone call from the organizer of the golf tournament. The donations for the evening silent auction were to have been delivered that morning, but no one could track them down. Rachel glanced at the clock and sighed. Lorna and Reuben were gone for the day. She was on her own.

She phoned Mrs. Simpson and explained the situation, trying not to let the woman's clipped replies add to her burden of guilt. She was efficient, Rachel reminded herself as she hung up the phone. That was why the woman talked the way she did. It did not mean that Rachel was neglecting Gracie. Not at all.

Nonetheless it was eight o'clock by the time she was heading back up to her condo. She had a few more phone calls to make before she was done for the night. Gracie would probably be asleep by the time she got there anyhow—she would have time.

But as she got off the elevator she heard Gracie's cries coming through the doorway of her apartment. Déjà vu.

As she entered the condo, Mrs. Simpson got up from the couch with Gracie and handed the crying toddler over to Rachel with undue haste. The tight set of her jaw and her narrowed eyes showed the woman's displeasure.

"I understood that I would be working regular hours," Mrs. Simpson said, picking up her coat and purse, which had been lying ready on the couch. "I cannot work these hours continually."

Could this woman be any starchier? Where had Pilar found her?

Rachel looked down at Gracie, who clung to her with damp chubby hands, wondering how Mrs. Simpson had dealt with the girl. Thankfully Gracie had stopped crying and was only sniffing now. Again Rachel felt a flush of guilt for leaving her alone. Clearly Gracie felt comfortable only around her. Which put a definite crimp in Rachel's life.

"Unfortunately I don't know when I'm going to be leaving and when I'm going to be home," Rachel said, trying to pacify her. She really could not afford to get this woman riled up. "I understood from Pilar—"

"If you cannot guarantee me *regular* working hours," Mrs. Simpson said, cutting her off, "I am afraid we shall have to revisit our agreement." She buttoned up her coat and, it seemed, her lips.

The frustration of the day spilled over. "I'm not renegotiating," Rachel snapped. "If you can't work the hours I need you to work, then maybe you better quit."

Mrs. Simpson lifted her chin enough to show Rachel what she thought of her, then swept out of the apartment without another word.

Chapter Seven

"The doctor said it would take that long?" Rachel twisted a strand of hair around and around her finger, wincing as she pulled it just a little too tight. "How is Mom with that?"

"Impatient," Charles said. "But she is so thankful that you are taking care of Gracie."

Rachel pushed aside a filing box with her foot as she dropped into her father's chair. She pushed down a flurry of panic at the thought of all the work she had to get done in the next couple of months. The Noble Foundation Picnic was looming on top of her usual management duties and her own personal files. Moving her files back to her parents' place would make her busier, but it was easier on Gracie to be back in her familiar setting.

"Well, so far it's going okay," she said with a false heartiness. Her father had enough on his mind; he didn't need to know that the past few days she had felt as if she was barely holding on to her life. She just needed to catch a new rhythm. Work a little harder. She could catch up if only she could get a few more hours in at night.

She and her father exchanged more pleasantries, and Rachel promised to try to come and visit as soon as she had some time.

As she hung up she dropped her head against the back of her father's chair. Time was getting to be an even more precious commodity than before Gracie. And she hadn't had a lot of it then.

She dragged her hands over her face as her mind worried at her current problem. Too much to do. Too little time. Too many responsibilities. She should be farther along planning the picnic than she was. She needed to get LaReese settled. Needed to get Reuben and Lorna on track, and a myriad of other smaller responsibilities that she could not dump on just anyone. She had been taking care of things herself so long, she could not imagine passing any of the responsibilities on.

As her mind whirled through all the work that needed doing, one of her mother's phrases sifted through her mind. "Let go and let God."

Rachel let the phrase settle a moment, as if trying it on. The offer was tempting. If Rachel trusted God, that is…

She sucked in a long slow breath, retied her ponytail and pushed herself up from the chair. No, she was better off taking care of things herself. That way she had control.

Just as she was about to go back to her car for another box, the telephone rang again. Rachel checked the call display and picked up the receiver.

"Hey, Lorna, what can I do for you?" She glanced at the clock. Gracie was due to wake up from her nap soon and Rachel wanted to get her car unloaded before that happened.

"I don't want to be a bother, but I just got a call from Reuben. He is on the road and wants me to access a bunch of files."

"What files?" Rachel asked, tucking the phone between her shoulder and her chin as she booted up her father's computer. Lorna gave her the names, and Rachel frowned. "He hasn't been working on those."

"I know. I looked for them but couldn't find them." Lorna paused, as if she wanted to say more.

"That's because I have them here with me." Early this morning, Rachel had gone to the office and taken home what she thought she might need.

"Oh. I see. Well, you see, Reuben…well…he called and said he would be helping you with them and the one on LaReese Binet."

"Next time he asks, let him know I have those here and if he needs any information he can call me." Rachel tried to keep from sounding annoyed. "I made a list of things I would like you to do for me for the next few days. We'll keep in touch by phone or e-mail."

"Do you want me to send you files from your computer?"

"No. I've got one of the computer techs to set my computer up so I can access it from here via the Internet."

"I could have sent you what you needed if you gave me your password," Lorna said, her tone slightly aggrieved.

"This works just fine." She had too much private information on the computer, and though she was sure Lorna was discreet, she did not want the information to go beyond her. "Anyhow, I better go. Call me if you need anything."

As she hung up the phone something niggled. What was

Reuben doing? She had made it very clear which files she wanted him to work on.

She listened for Gracie, but was relieved to hear nothing. Then she picked up the phone and dialed Reuben's cell number.

No answer. She frowned as she laid the handset in the cradle, drumming her fingers in impatience on the desk. Obviously she wasn't going to get any answers at the moment.

She ran back to her car for the next set of boxes, each time pausing to see if Gracie was awake. When Rachel had laid her down for her nap the child had snuggled into her crib. Her smile of utter contentment had made the trouble of the move worthwhile. And knowing that the housekeeper was around most of the day gave Rachel some badly needed backup.

She tried Reuben's number again, once again getting no reply, which puzzled her. He usually had his cell phone on all the time. She left a terse message for him to call her, then got back to work.

But all the while, doubts about Reuben crept around the edges of her mind, creating an uneasiness she could not dispel. She could not get rid of the idea that he was up to something. Or the idea that it involved LaReese Binet.

"So are you telling me you have decided not to go with the Foundation?" Rachel asked, tucking the phone under her chin as she wiped Gracie's face and hands with the wet cloth she had learned to keep in readiness by her computer. This morning Gracie had discovered the plants in her father's study. Friday it was a bottle of syrup.

Since Rachel had moved her and her office back home,

two things had happened. Rachel's work life got more hectic and unorganized, and in spite of Rachel's busyness, Gracie settled down. She was happier and, as a result, more active.

"I understand, LaReese," Rachel was saying as the same unsettled feeling she'd had all week clutched at her. "It is your money to dispose of as you please. Just as with purchasing something, I want to make sure you get the best value for your money. There are a lot of questionable charities around."

"Well, that young person from your office came by with some information on a real interesting group," La-Reese was saying. "Something to do with children and prison."

Rachel frowned, her unease growing into a full-blown worry-fest. Reuben was gone, checking the credentials of that self-same group. But he wasn't answering his phone, so she really had no idea where he was. He must be dealing in the background with LaReese.

"I hate to pester you, but I would really like to come over once more," Rachel said. "To talk things over with you before you make a decision."

LaReese sighed. "All right, though I wish the Foundation would make up its mind. Come by on Sunday at two-thirty."

Rachel frowned at the dial tone now buzzing in her ear. What did LaReese mean by the Foundation making up its mind?

And where was Reuben?

She bit her lip, the nervousness she had felt before increasing. Things were not going well, and she had the feeling of holding onto threads that were slowly slipping out of her grasp.

If she believed it would make a difference, she might pray. *Let go and let God.*

Rachel pushed that thought aside. She had not spent much time with God lately. So talking to Him whenever it worked out only for her seemed a mite hypocritical.

Gracie toddled over to her side, and before Rachel could stop her, she got hold of the mouse and yanked.

The cable went taut. Gracie kept pulling. The mouse slipped out of her hand and she fell backward with a muffled thump. She sat there with a surprised expression on her face and then took a deep breath and started howling.

Of course the doorbell would ring right now. Why not?

"You're okay, little one," she said with a frown. But Gracie would not be consoled. Picking Gracie up and shifting her weight so the child rested more easily on one hip, Rachel strode through the house to the front door, wondering who would be coming on a Saturday to her parents' place.

She yanked the door open.

Eli. Again.

He stood on her front step, his helmet resting under one arm, his other hand in the front pocket of his blue jeans.

"What do you want?" she asked over the sounds of Gracie's wails.

As soon as she said the words, she regretted them. She hadn't meant to sound so combative. The agitation that swirled around her in his presence was an unfamiliar emotion she didn't know how to deal with.

Plus Gracie was crying, and once again Eli was witness to it.

"I'm sorry," she said more quietly, trying to shush her

sister. "It's just…" She let the sentence trail off, then stood back, pulling the door wider open for him. "Please come in. I'm sorry I snapped. I'm feeling a little frazzled right now. I have to confess that's an unfamiliar feeling for me." She pushed the hair that had come loose from her ponytail back from her face, suddenly aware of her bare feet, frayed blue jeans and ratty T-shirt. After Gracie had ruined two of her blouses and gotten ink on one of her best suits, she had given up on office attire.

Gracie drew in a shaky breath, let out a halfhearted cry and then reached out to Eli. He set his helmet on a delicate table that flanked the wide glass doors of the foyer and took Gracie in his arms.

"How is she doing?" Eli asked, pulling back to look at her. He laid the back of his hand against her forehead, then smiled. "Hey, Gracie, except for those tears in your eyes, you are just fine." He rubbed them away with his thumb in a fatherly gesture.

"She *is* fine," Rachel insisted, feeling a tad defensive. Why was Eli coming around again? She was doing all the things she was supposed to. If she needed his help or advice she would have called him. "She's crying because she's miffed that my mouse won't come and play with her."

Eli gave her a puzzled smile. A smile which, in spite of her momentary pique with him, made her feel fluttery.

"She fell trying to pull my computer mouse off my desk," Rachel explained, tucking her hands in the back pockets of her blue jeans.

"I see," he said, a grin developing. He brushed the curls back from Gracie's face and set her on the floor. "Well, little lady, you better learn to control that temper of yours."

Gracie wavered a moment, caught her balance, then

toddled off down the hall to the playroom her parents had made for her just off the kitchen, one arm tucked against her body, the other spread out to balance her hitching step.

"And how are you doing?" Eli asked, turning his attention back to Rachel.

She blew out her breath and shook her head. "I don't know if I'm cut out to be a mother," she said ruefully. "I can't keep up to her. I can't imagine what she would be like if she was a normal toddler."

"Gracie *is* normal," Eli said. "She is just facing a few more challenges than other kids."

Rachel felt her cheeks burn. The single word, spoken without thinking, made her feel insensitive. "I meant, if she had all her capacities," she said, a defensive note creeping into her voice. "What else am I supposed to say about her?" she said, the frustration of the past few days spilling out. "You were the one who told me yourself how I had to change my life to work around her disabilities. You were the one who said if I'm not careful, she could end up in the hospital. So if she's normal, why am I doing all this? Moving my office from downtown to my parents' place? Trying to juggle taking care of her and working? Trying to keep everything going?" Her voice grew more agitated with each sentence.

As the last word reverberated in the spacious foyer of the house, Rachel felt the fight sift out of her. Eli didn't bother to hide the surprise on his face.

"I'm sensing a subtext to all of this…text," he said carefully.

"I'm sorry," she said, raising her hands in a gesture of surrender. "It's just that the past few days have been crazy. Things are happening at the Foundation I can't control and

I'm not used to taking care of a child who needs to be periodically dunked in cold water."

Eli burst out laughing, a pair of matching dimples winking out from beside his mouth. "I'm sorry," he said, taking a quick breath. "Did you have to do it again?"

"No. Thank goodness." Rachel felt the tension that had held her in its tenacious grip the past few days loosen in the face of Eli's humor. "She's been delightfully healthy since I came back here." She glanced over her shoulder at Gracie, who was now dragging around one of Rachel's shoes. "It pains me to say this," she said, giving Eli a cautious smile, "but you were right about her. She just needed to be home."

"And with someone she knew," Eli added softly. "In spite of what you may think, she does seem to have formed an attachment to you."

A gentle silence drifted between them. As it lengthened, Rachel felt a faint tug of something indefinable. As if under its own power, her gaze lifted toward him and she caught him looking at her, his expression suddenly serious.

She had an urge to lean on him. To rest her head against his shoulder and just let him take over her life.

She swayed a moment, then caught herself. *Silly girl. You are on your own. It's the only way you stay in control.*

"Well…" She stopped, cleared her throat and tried again. "Thanks for coming. I'm sorry if I sounded a bit, well, out of sorts. I've been crazy busy."

Eli gave her a careful smile. "I think it's great that you are willing to take care of your sister, you know."

His quietly spoken words settled over the uneasiness she had felt since Gracie charged into her life. Gave her a feeling of approbation.

"Thank you. I, uh, haven't been the most willing. And I have to confess she still scares me a little…"

"Hey, at least you're honest about it." He took a step back and retrieved his helmet from the table. "Well, I gotta run. I was on my way to the hospital to check on some tests we ran yesterday and thought I would see how you were doing."

Rachel nodded, surprised at the regret that spiraled through her. "Okay, then. Thanks for stopping by."

Eli hesitated as if about to say something. Then he ducked his head, turned and left.

Rachel felt a warmth, kindled by Eli's approval, curl through her. For a moment she let it flow, grow.

The sound of his motorcycle roaring away was like a dash of cold water. A reminder of the pain of loving. She was heading down a path she had thought she would never travel again, and as the roar of the motorcycle faded into the distance she felt the fanciful feelings she had momentarily indulged in fade away, as well.

He hadn't come for her, she reminded herself. He had come for Gracie. He had come to make sure Rachel was doing her job.

But even as she talked herself into that, a curious thought circled lightly and landed.

He could have called to see how Gracie was doing.

And right behind that came another.

The plantation was not at all on his way to the hospital..

Chapter Eight

Well, that was brilliant, Eli thought as he twisted his wrist and kicked the motorcycle into a higher gear. He leaned into the curve of the long driveway of the Noble Plantation, then slowed for the last corner.

As he headed down the road toward the hospital he sped up. The wind rushing past his face could not rid him of the notion that he had just made a colossal fool of himself in front of Rachel Noble. He had only meant to see how she was managing at home with Gracie. The visit was strictly as Gracie's doctor.

Doing it at her plantation home did not help much, either. What in the world had he been thinking?

Right now, he was thinking of how cute she looked with her hair slightly loose and wearing a faded T-shirt. He was thinking of how approachable she seemed in her bare feet and blue jeans.

And he was thinking of that huge home she lived in. And how much money her parents had. And how he was sure that in spite of their easy and relaxed airs, her parents had someone in mind for her. Someone who had a known past.

What Eli knew about his parents could be written on the palm of his hand. The same hand that still held the scar from the accident that took them from him.

Peggy and Tyrone did not often talk about his parents or encourage him to find out more. As a young man he had not understood this. Now, he realized that it probably was partly a self-defense mechanism for them.

He tried to imagine Gracie wanting to know about her own mother, a woman who had treated her with such disregard, when the Nobles had done so much for her.

Thinking of Gracie brought him squarely back to Rachel. How the wisps of dark hair framed her face, brought out the brown tints in her hazel eyes. He wondered what her hair looked like down, flowing over her shoulders. He was fairly sure it was long, silky.

With a start he pulled himself back to the present. Rachel Noble was out of his league.

Rachel carefully wiped the remnants of Sunday morning breakfast from Gracie's face with a damp cloth. She set her on the floor, wiped down her high chair and turned just in time to see Gracie toddle off toward the patio doors. Aleeda always kept the windows sparkling clean but since she left for the weekend, Gracie's hand prints already decorated the glass.

At first Rachel had tried to wipe up behind her, but when Gracie slapped her pudgy hands against the glass for the third time, Rachel gave up.

Rachel cleaned up the breakfast dishes and rescued a ficus from Gracie's inquisitive hands. Put the dishes in the dishwasher and pulled Gracie down from a chair she was trying to climb. Wiped the counters and Gracie's high chair and took away a fork that Rachel had forgotten to load in the dishwasher and that Gracie had found on a chair.

How did people with more than one child survive?

"So, Gracie," she said with more confidence than she felt. "What do we do next?"

She looked at the clock, then back at the girl. She knew her parents normally went to church on Sunday. When she was young she always went, but after Keith, she had stayed away. Even since she was back in town, the only time she had been to church was to attend Meg and Jared's wedding.

She knew it was a huge disappointment to her parents, but she no longer felt she had to do things simply because they expected it. She was living her own life, and God had not been a part of it.

As she looked at Gracie, though, she suddenly felt an extra responsibility. Sure she was only two, but while Rachel felt she could make decisions about her faith for herself, she did not feel right about doing the same for this child.

But her parent's house created its own memories and history of Sunday. Work had always been frowned upon on Sunday.

"So, Gracie, do you want to go to church?" she asked, rinsing out the cloth and laying it to dry on the rack inside the cupboard door.

"Go church. Go church," Gracie said, bobbing up and down.

Rachel didn't have the time, but her work was making

her feel as if she was going in circles. Besides, after being housebound for a couple of days, she desperately needed to get out.

Half an hour later Rachel stood in the back of the church, hoping to spot either Pilar, or Meg and her husband. She had seen the twins when she brought Gracie to the nursery.

Gracie had seemed more than happy to toddle around, playing with the toys and the other children. It was a familiar setting for her, Rachel realized when she gave the attendant Gracie's bag. Gracie had her own cubbyhole with her name on it. She was given a name tag that was clipped to the back of her dress. *Gracie Noble.*

Rachel had felt a touch of melancholy when she saw that. It reminded her that her parents had brought her to this church to a young girls' club, and when she was older, to a youth group. She had been an active participant up until after her college graduation.

Until Keith.

And now, as she looked around the sanctuary, memories flashed through her mind with painful clarity. Memories that had not arisen during Meg's wedding. Somehow that intimate ceremony had not brought them out so clearly as the rustle of people filling the pews, the murmur of conversation, the early morning sun slanting into the sanctuary through the stained-glass windows.

She remembered singing with Pilar and Meg. Goofing around during youth group. Listening to speakers. Looking across the sanctuary to see Keith—wondering if he had noticed her. Their romance had begun here, as young students of middle school, then on to high school and college. There was hardly a memory of church that did not have memories of Keith attached to it.

When she came back from New York, the pain was still fresh, her feeling of abandonment from God still strong. So she had stayed away.

Until now.

But to her surprise, as her gaze wandered over the familiar setting, only a gentle pain came on the heels of memories that had, at one time, brought wrenching sorrow.

What was even more surprising, for a moment, she could not even remember what Keith looked like.

The realization gave her pause. She had stored most of Keith's pictures at her parents' place after his death and hadn't looked at them since. It had hurt too much. She wondered how she would feel now.

Finally, she spotted Pilar sitting by her parents, Salvador and Rita Estes. Pilar was reading a piece of paper, frowning at it, as Rachel slipped into the pew beside her.

"I thought going to church made you happy," Rachel murmured, leaning sideways.

Pilar blinked, then almost laughed out loud. "Rachel. What are you doing here?" she asked as she gave her friend a quick hug.

"I felt I should bring Gracie," Rachel said.

Pilar's smile slipped a notch as if she was hoping for another reason. "Well, I'm glad you are here." She gave Rachel's silky hair a casual flick with her index finger. "And I'm glad you wore your hair down for a change. I really like it."

"It came loose while I was getting Gracie dressed and I didn't have time to fix it," she said, self-consciously smoothing her hair back.

Rachel glanced around the church, taking in the solidity of the aged wooden pews, the wooden pulpit, the stained-glass windows. They gave the church a warm and welcoming glow that called back many Sundays and memories of moments of peace and happiness that slipped past the wall of resistance she had built to God and this place.

"Rachel. Good to see you again." Rita Estes had spotted her and leaned across Pilar to greet her. Rita wore her salt-and-pepper black hair in an elegant bob that accented the large gold hoops hanging from her ears. Her bright smile and sparkling eyes called back other good memories. "I'm so thankful you could come."

Rachel smiled back. "It is good to be here again." And as she spoke the words, she realized she meant them.

As Rita turned to her daughter to ask a question, Rachel looked back around the sanctuary.

Sandra Lange sat a few seats ahead of them, her head bowed, her folded hands pressed to her chin. She looked as if she was praying. Rachel watched her, remembering Sandra's enigmatic comments of last Sunday, wondering what she had meant by them.

Mayor Gerald Morrow and his wife Lindsay sat one row in front of Sandra. He sat ramrod straight, looking ahead as if honoring God with his presence here. Rachel had dealt with him from time to time through her work. She respected him, yet was always thankful he was not an adversary of hers.

As if in gentle counterpoint to the tough air he always exuded, Lindsay, his wife, sat close to him. As she bent her head to read the same paper he was reading, her thick black hair swung over her narrow cheekbone, a dark contrast to her husband's white hair. As Rachel watched, Lindsay looked up at her husband and tucked her arm through his. Her affection toward her husband made Rachel feel melancholy. As a young girl she had always imagined sitting with her husband in church, book-ended by children.

Her dream husband had always been Keith.

Unbidden came the thought of Eli stopping by the plantation house on his motorcycle. His gentle smile when he encouraged her. His presence should have made her feel resentful, but she couldn't dredge up the emotion. Instead, she found herself thinking of him more and more. Wondering when he would "stop by" again.

"I don't know if we are going to be able to make our brunch date," Pilar said, her voice breaking into her thoughts.

Rachel jumped.

"Okay, where were you with that dreamy look on your face?" Pilar asked, her gaze piercing Rachel's as if trying to get into her mind.

"Just…well…just remembering," Rachel said, trying to gather up her scattered thoughts. "What did you say about brunch?"

Pilar gave her a look that clearly conveyed her disbelief, but to Rachel's relief she didn't push the issue. "Meg said Jared is busy with something and Anne isn't feeling good, so we won't be meeting this Sunday."

"That's fine," Rachel replied. "I was thinking of picking up some sandwiches from the diner and going to the park with Gracie anyway."

"Winchester Park?" Pilar asked with a knowing smile. "Think you might catch a football game while you're at it?"

Rachel pretended innocence, even though she knew precisely what Pilar was getting at. "I just might."

Pilar was about to say something else when Reverend John Fraser stepped up to the pulpit. He glanced around the congregation, his eyes glinting behind his wire-rim glasses.

He welcomed the congregation, and as they got to their feet to sing the first set of songs, he encouraged people to take a moment to greet one another.

Rachel shook hands with an unfamiliar couple in front of her, an old classmate behind her. She caught a quick movement to her left and saw Sandra Lange extend her hand to Mayor Morrow. But Mayor Morrow wasn't looking at her.

Lindsay Morrow was, but she didn't shake Sandra's hand, either. Then, with an enigmatic smile, Sandra lowered her hand and looked up at Pastor Fraser.

Curiouser and curiouser, thought Rachel, wondering what that was all about.

But she didn't have time to wonder. The first song came up on the screen overhead, and as a youthful worship band struck up a tune, the congregation slipped into song.

The words were unfamiliar to Rachel, but the tune was upbeat and catchy and by the second verse she was singing along. She had always enjoyed singing, and other than church or the shower, she did not have much opportunity to do so.

The songs pulled her along as the lyrics became more meaningful and the songs a little slower, as if drawing the congregation away from the busyness of every day life toward worship.

By the time the last note died down, Rachel felt a curious energy flowing through her, lifting her up. She felt her familiar resistance to God, but at the same time, being in this church where she had some history, brought back an earlier connection to God.

Reverend Fraser started preaching, his mellow voice drawing out older memories of other church services. She couldn't help but listen. He moved from anecdote to application drawing Rachel along. His sermon was about control. Something Rachel hadn't found since Gracie came into her life.

"…and so we can resent what God is doing in our lives. What He has been trying to teach us. We can try to ignore God, but to do that is like trying to get rid of light by writing the word 'darkness' on the wall. We may be hurting and in trouble, but, as C. S. Lewis says, 'God whispers to us in our pleasures, speaks in our conscience, but shouts in our pains: it is His megaphone to rouse a deaf world.' Our pain and sorrow becomes His way, I believe, of getting our attention. And I believe He needs to because we think we are self-sufficient creatures. We think we can do everything on our own. We think we can live apart from God, which is like the scent of the flower trying to separate itself from the flower. God is always there and He is waiting for us to give over the control of our lives to Him."

And in those few words, the reverend had captured Rachel's confusion. When Keith died, she had stopped her ears to what God may have had to say to her. She had felt the best way to live was on her own. To be in charge and in control.

In the past few days, the events of her life had shown her how futile that was.

But what else was she supposed to do? She was doing good things at the Foundation. People and charities depended on her work. She couldn't simply surrender control of that. She had hoped to slowly move Reuben into a position of more responsibility, but because of the strangeness of his actions the past few weeks, she might even have to think about letting him go.

A thread of fear wrapped itself around her heart. Right now, more than ever, she needed people she could count on.

And she didn't know where she could find them. Rachel was pulled back to the moment by Reverend Fraser's words.

"…so how do we get ourselves so wound up? By thinking we are in charge of our lives, when really, we aren't.

"Sometimes God lets us go our own way to let us find out for ourselves that our souls are restless until they turn to Him. So now I want to close with the words of the Psalmist from Psalm 139. 'If I settle on the far side of the sea, even there Your hand will guide me, Your right hand will hold me fast.'"

The words resonated through the building and came to rest in Rachel's heart. She had turned her back on God. She didn't trust Him. And yet, in spite of that, she had never been able to subdue completely a vague restlessness in her. She had never been able to say without any doubts, that God did not exist.

Yes, she still mourned Keith's death. Yes, thinking of how she lost him still made her feel vulnerable. She still wondered why God had not answered her prayers. She didn't know the answer to that. No one would.

But she knew she could not deny God's presence in her life as easily as she had. She had felt His familiar touch today. It had brought back memories of a time when she was closer to Him. When she had struggled to serve Him in everything she did.

She also realized that her work at the Noble Foundation recognized God's challenge that she wasn't on this world to serve herself.

As the service wound down, she felt herself return to reality. She needed to assimilate what she had just discovered, think it through, and she knew she couldn't do that if she stayed to talk.

As the last song was sung, she slipped out of the pew, avoiding Pilar and anyone else she knew.

An hour later, Rachel pulled Gracie's stroller out of the car and settled her in it. She draped the diaper bag over the handles, double-checked to make sure she had everything, and then headed off down the shaded asphalt path that wound along the edge of the park. As she walked, she let the quiet of the park, the warmth of the sunshine and the whisper of the leaves on the trees surround her.

In the distance she could hear children laughing. The shouts of a group of men. And for the moment she felt anonymous.

"Hello, hello," Gracie cooed at passersby as they walked.

Everyone who saw her smiled as she dispensed her easy charm. Once in a while someone would stop and bend over to talk to her. Then she would curl her head away, almost coyly, and blink her long eyelashes. Rachel had to laugh. So young and already flirtatious.

Rachel ambled along, content simply to follow the path. She had much on her mind and much to absorb. This morning she had once again felt God's presence, His love. And it called to emotions from her past that had always been there, even before Keith. To her surprise, being in church, hearing God's word being spoken, singing praises to Him, had opened up a space she had closed off completely. She still wasn't sure she was ready to let go as fully as she had been encouraged to do, but maybe she was willing to give God a second chance. When she had the time.

"Heads up!"

The loud warning cry accomplished what it was supposed to. Rachel's head snapped up—

Just in time to see a football sailing toward her. She ducked and spun Gracie's stroller around to protect her.

The ball fell harmlessly in the grass a few feet from her, and she straightened in time to see Eli jogging toward her. Again he was wearing blue jeans. But today he wore a T-shirt. He scooped up the ball, then turned to her just as she came to face him.

"Sorry about that," he said. Then a huge grin split his face as he recognized her. "Hey there, Rachel. I didn't expect to see you here."

Rachel may have forgotten about Eli's Sunday afternoon football game. But she hadn't forgotten the soft green of his eyes and his crooked half-smile. Nor how tall he was as even in his bare feet he topped her in her shoes by a good six inches.

"Hey, yourself," she said quietly, feeling curiously breathless.

"Eli. Eli," Gracie called out, lifting her hands up to him.

Eli bent down to Gracie. "How are you doing, princess?" he asked, tucking a curl behind her ear. "Are you being a good girl for Rachel?"

"Go church," she said, clapping her hands.

Eli glanced up at her, lifting one eyebrow as if questioning her.

"I thought I should," she said with a light shrug. "I know my parents always bring her."

"And how was Reverend Fraser this morning?" Eli stood up, tapping the football against the side of his leg.

Rachel held his gaze, sensing a mild mocking tone in his voice. "Actually, he was very good."

Eli seemed to pick up on her sincerity. "That's good." He pointed the football at the large bag hanging from the handles of the stroller. "You figure on being gone for a couple of weeks?"

Rachel laughed. "No. I packed a snack for me and Gracie. Just coffee, milk and cookies. I was looking for a nice quiet place to eat it."

"There's a group of tables tucked under some trees a ten-minute walk from here. There's a playground close by for Gracie. I could show you if you like."

Rachel didn't think it would be that hard to find. As far as she knew there was only one path that wound through the park, but at the same time, she sensed an unspoken invitation in his offer.

"That would be nice."

Eli batted the football against his other hand. "Just let me get rid of this and get my sneakers back on and I'll show you."

Rachel nodded, her gaze holding his as something almost palpable whispered between them. He took a few slow steps backward, then turned and jogged back to where his friends were waiting, calling out to him to hurry up.

Rachel drew in a slow breath, feeling for a moment as if she was allowing herself to head down a completely different path. She watched as Eli joined his friends. She saw him hand the football over to a tall man with dark hair. She heard laughter as he retrieved his sneakers, then the whole group looked across the open grass to her, and her cheeks burned. It was like high school crushes all over again.

This was a mistake, she thought, yet she was reluctant to move. It would be over in a few minutes, she told herself. It would be good to spend some time with Eli. She could ask him a few more questions about Gracie.

Gracie wiggled in the stroller as they waited. "Want to go. Go now."

"We will, sweetie," Rachel said, rocking the stroller to settle her down.

Finally Eli was walking across the grass toward them. His friends were still laughing but Eli was pointedly ignoring them.

And as he came closer, Rachel felt it again. The hint of attraction. The whisper of a promise. She wanted to ignore it. To push it aside.

But when Eli smiled at her, she found she couldn't.

Chapter Nine

"So how has Gracie been?" Eli kept the question casual. Tried not to sound like a doctor when he asked it.

"So far so good."

Rachel kept her eyes on the path, which was a good thing, because Eli had a hard time keeping his eyes off her. She wore her hair loose again and it was like a swath of gleaming silk flowing over her shoulders and down her back.

"It looks like the ear infection is going away," Rachel continued. "At least she hasn't had any more fevers."

"That's good."

And that was lame.

Unfortunately he couldn't think of anything profound to say at the moment, so he sauntered alongside her, trying to look more confident than he felt.

If he was honest with himself, there was something about this woman made him feel gauche. He usually didn't have a hard time talking to women, and though he dated occasionally, he had never allowed anything serious to develop. He preferred order to his life, and at this point, he didn't feel he was ready to pursue a serious relationship.

He wasn't sure why he was pursuing Rachel now. She wasn't the kind of woman he would normally be attracted to. But in spite of his initial negative impression, she stayed in his thoughts with a tenacity that surprised him. He tried to be practical and analytical about his attraction to her. Tried to dissect it. Tried to analyze the feelings away. He wasn't ready for someone serious in his life. He wasn't where he wanted to be.

He glanced sidelong at her. And caught her doing the same to him.

She didn't look away, and he couldn't, either.

"So how is your work going?" He had to ask about that, if he was going for casual. That would be the normal thing to ask about, right?

Rachel couldn't stop the faint sigh that escaped her lips. "I have been trying to meet with a client for the past week and she's been evading me. We are having a hard time connecting her with a charity that she can get excited about."

"Is that part of what you do for the Foundation? All I know is that your parents are very proud of what you've done there." It was that pride that had created a curiosity in him to meet this woman that Beatrice and Charles Noble talked so much about. He wanted to know more about her. What she did. Who she really was.

Because in spite of his initial reaction to her, she intrigued him.

Rachel gave him a quick sidelong look. "You really want to know?"

He returned her puzzled look with a smile. "Yes, I do."

So as they walked she explained what the Foundation did. How they set up fund-raising activities, how they monitored the nonprofit organizations that applied to the Foundation for money. As she talked she grew more animated, her hazel eyes sparkling, and Eli grew even more fascinated by her.

"The hospital is also supported by the Foundation on an ongoing basis," she was saying. "Though, we have had a problem with the cash flow lately."

"I understood from your parents that the Foundation was well endowed."

"For the most part it is, but lately we have had quite a few new charities starting up and asking for funds. All of these need to be investigated, which is also what we do for prospective clients who want to make sure their money is being used wisely and well. And for some strange reason, we've lost potential donors the past few months." She stopped herself and gave him an apologetic smile. "Sorry. I tend to start rambling when I talk about the Foundation."

"Not at all," he said. "It's always interesting to listen to someone talking about something they are passionate about."

Rachel gave a little laugh. "My friends seem to think I'm married to my job. They just don't understand how important the Foundation is to me. What working there has done for me." She looked up at him, her eyes shining with an intensity that called to his own dedication to his work.

And in that moment, he felt a spark of connection.

She was still looking at him when a movement caught his eye. He pulled his reluctant gaze away in time to see some young boys on bicycles bearing down on them full speed. Eli grabbed the buggy with one hand and caught Rachel's arm with the other. He dragged them both out of harm's way just in time to feel the breeze of the boys whizzing past them. A halfhearted apology drifted behind the boys as they sped away.

Rachel stopped, glanced back over her shoulder, then up at Eli. "What was that?"

"Teenagers," he said, suddenly reluctant to release her arm.

Rachel laughed at that, and if Eli was intrigued before, he was fully captivated now.

"I didn't even see them coming," she said, breathless now at their near miss. "Thanks for rescuing me."

Eli was still holding her arm, though not as tightly as he had when he pulled her away. And she was still looking at him.

Rachel was the first one to look away and then she slowly pulled her arm out of his hand. Her hair slipped over her face, hiding her expression.

"Here's the playground I was telling you about," Eli said.

"I have lots of coffee and an extra cup. Would you like to join us?" Rachel glanced up at him again, her lower lip caught between her teeth.

For a moment she looked like an unsure schoolgirl, which gave Eli enough encouragement to accept.

He helped Gracie out of the buggy while Rachel took out the Thermos and the cups. Gracie wriggled loose from him and toddled off to the playground. Now and again she would look back over her shoulder, as if to make sure they were still watching her.

"Is she always going to have that hesitation in her

walk?" Rachel asked, watching Gracie struggle to climb over a wooden board, the only barrier between her and the sandbox.

Eli nodded, watching her, as well. He sat down beside Rachel, facing the sandbox so they could keep an eye on Gracie. "Unfortunately the only thing we can do for her is try to make sure she doesn't lose what mobility she has in her arm and leg."

"Will it get worse?"

"Hopefully not." He smiled as if to reassure her. "But overall, she's a happy girl."

"She is now." Rachel laid the napkins on the table side by side. "I know how nasty other girls can be. Once she reaches middle school, it can get pretty brutal."

"What makes you say that?" Eli was surprised at the muted anger in her voice.

"What happened to my friend, Anne," Rachel said. "The horrible teasing she endured because she was a bit 'different.' I don't want to see it happen to Gracie."

Eli laid his hand on her shoulder with a light touch. "It doesn't have to happen that way," he said quietly.

She looked up at him. "I suppose not. But since I started taking care of her, I can't believe how defensive I am starting to feel for her."

"When I first met you, you seemed uncomfortable around her."

Rachel lifted one shoulder in a casual shrug as she looked away. "I was."

"Why?"

Rachel bit her lip, hesitating, then looked back at him. To his surprise, Eli saw pain in her eyes.

"It doesn't matter."

"Why do you say that?"

"It's part of my past. A part I'm trying to forget."

"The past is hard to let go of," Eli said. He should know. He had struggled himself with memories of his natural parents. He was six when they died and still remembered them. When he came to the Cavanaughs, they didn't seem to know what to do about the hurt in his life. So they didn't talk about it. "Whether we like it or not it is part of who we are."

Rachel sighed lightly, glancing back again at Gracie. "I know it has been a large part of who I am, yet I feel like that's changing."

Eli heard the pain in her voice. "Is this something to do with why you hate hospitals?"

Rachel nodded, half turning away from him. For a moment he thought she wasn't going to answer him. But then she pulled her knees up to her chin, wrapped her arms around them and started talking.

"I spent a month in the hospital eight years ago," she said, her voice so quiet that Eli had to strain to hear her. "I sat at the bedside of the young man I thought God had destined for me to marry. For four weeks, I prayed for his recovery. I know too well how a respirator sounds, the beep of a heart monitor. But my prayers didn't make a difference…"

Her voice hitched on the last word, and Eli understood where the story was going. He brushed aside his uncertain feelings toward her and covered her hand with his in a gesture of sympathy.

To his surprise, she curled her fingers around his, clinging to him, and as she did, a place slowly opened deep in his heart.

"The first time I saw Gracie was in the hospital. I couldn't help make the connection."

She looked up at him and Eli was surprised to see a single tear slide silently down her cheek. He took his other hand and gently wiped it away. "I'm sorry," he whispered. "I didn't know."

Rachel drew in a shuddering breath, then looked down at their linked hands. "You don't need to be sorry. I was making bad conclusions." She sniffed and glanced back over her shoulder to where Gracie was playing. To Eli's disappointment, she pulled her hand away from his and walked toward Gracie.

When she came back she was talking to the child, avoiding his gaze, but Eli didn't care. He realized that in these past few moments she had shown him a part of herself he suspected few people saw.

"Can you push her buggy closer to the table and lock the wheels?" Rachel asked, in control now. "She'll eat better if she's sitting down."

As she set Gracie down in the buggy, Eli poured the coffee, a mixture of feelings swirling through him. He wanted to find out more about Keith. Wanted to find out more about Rachel. But he knew that he had to follow her lead. So he switched to the ordinary.

"The coffee smells good."

Rachel handed Gracie a cookie and took her cup from Eli with a smile of thanks. She rested her elbows on the table and slowly inhaled the scent of the coffee.

"I was thinking about this all morning in church," she said, then took a careful sip.

"You don't usually go to church, do you?" Eli asked.

Rachel shook her head as she set her cup down, avoiding his gaze. "No. God and I haven't seen eye to eye for some time now."

"So given that, what made you go to church this morning?"

He felt as if he had to know. He used to go himself. He could understand why she would turn her back on God after such a disappointment. His own disappointment, his parents' death, had been much, much longer ago. He still harbored resentment over it, resentment that had grown when he was a teenager. And again, when he discovered that his adoptive parents had stopped him from asking questions about them, had held back pictures of them.

"A couple of things," she said softly. She looked over at Gracie who was kicking her feet, happily munching on a cookie. "I felt responsible for Gracie, and being at my parents' place…" She shrugged. "Whenever I stayed at Mom and Dad's I was expected to go to church. Hard to get rid of the feeling that I should. So I went. And to my surprise, I enjoyed it. I had a feeling that even though I rejected God, He hadn't rejected me. That was a very interesting revelation for me. Now I feel like I have to do something with it and I'm not sure what."

Eli watched the play of emotions over her face as she spoke. And found, as she talked about what the church service had done for her, as her face reflected a momentary peace, that he felt a surprising flicker of envy. Once he, too, had gone to church. To his parents' sorrow, he hadn't bothered once he'd moved out of the house.

His passion for his work had insidiously eaten away at his time away from the hospital. He had started staying at the clinic late on Friday evenings to catch up on work. Then it became Saturday mornings. Which meant his only day off was Sunday and even then he was often on call. So Sunday became synonymous with sleeping in and trying to find a way to maintain some kind of social life. Church was slowly eased out of his life.

As his passion for medicine increased, his faith had become lukewarm. Neither hot nor cold.

But as he listened to Rachel's hesitant seeking, he felt a faint stirring in his own heart. A calling to a faith he had felt in his past.

He took a sip of coffee as he rested his elbows on the table. He asked her a few more questions and their conversation easily moved from work to family. He discovered that, like him, she had been raised in a Christian home. Like him, her job had slowly taken her away from her upbringing. Like him, she had no outside hobbies.

She asked him about his parents. So he told her about the Cavanaughs. And his natural parents.

"Do you still remember them?" Rachel asked, leaning over to wipe Gracie's hands with a moist towelette.

"I was six when they were killed in a car accident." Eli glanced down at the scar that ran across the back of his hand. "I was an only child and the only one that survived."

"So you've known sadness, too."

Her face held a gentle recognition of his pain that called to him. But he shrugged her concern aside. "It was a long time ago."

"Yes. But they were your natural parents." She glanced at Gracie. "I know my mom and dad love this little girl dearly, but even at her age, she still comes to them as another person who already has some history. I imagine if you were six years old, you would have some very strong memories of your parents."

"Memories the Cavanaughs didn't really want me to bring up much," Eli said. He added a grin just so Rachel didn't think he was an ungrateful, maladjusted whiner.

"That's interesting. I wonder if it was a bit of jealousy. I know Mom and Dad had really mixed feelings about Gracie's mother coming to visit. In spite of how generous they are, when it came to Gracie they wanted to have her all to themselves." Rachel pulled Gracie out of the buggy, brushed the crumbs off her dress and carefully, helped her regain her balance. "They were actually a bit relieved when she decided to stay out of Gracie's life. And to tell you the truth, so was I." She watched Gracie as she worked her way around the picnic table, catching the wooden seat whenever she lost her balance in the grass.

Eli had never thought of that aspect before. "But my parents were dead. They were just memories."

"All the harder to fight. Memories stay in the background, changing according to your wishes. Getting better and kinder all the time." She shrugged. "But then, I don't know much about that. I'm blessed enough to still have my natural parents, goofs and all. I didn't have memories of other parents to fall back on when I was tired of the ones I had."

Her comment hit at some of the struggles he'd had as a young man. How often he'd run upstairs, frustrated with Peggy and Tyrone Cavanaugh, wishing he still had his own parents, the parents the Cavanaughs never wanted to talk about. The ones that would be "better." That would understand him more. Eli studied her. "You say you don't know much, but you've given me something else to think about. Something that makes sense."

Her smile drew his out. And as their gazes held, delving into each other, he felt as if he was standing on the verge of something unknown that would change his well-ordered life.

All he had to do was take that first step into the void. Away from the direction he had mapped out for himself as a young man angry with a confusing and messed-up world.

He didn't know if he dared. But as he held Rachel's gaze, he wasn't sure he could walk away, either. He wanted to see her again. Spend more time with her. He took a breath.

A beeping at his side made him jump. He glanced down at his pager and turned it off, resentment singing through him. And right on the heels of that resentment came a sense of relief at the rescue.

"Sorry. That's the hospital. I'm on call."

"Weren't you last week, as well?"

"I volunteered to cover for another doctor this weekend." He covered for some of the married doctors when they had things going on. He never minded working weekends. Now, he was thankful for the intrusion. He had set the course of his life quite clearly as a teenager. A relationship was not in the plans for a couple of years yet.

And yet…

"I understand," she said, but her smile had lost some of its luster.

Gracie had come back and was reaching out for Rachel to pick her up. Eli pushed himself up from the table as Rachel caught the child in her arms. "I hope it's not too serious."

"I guess I'll see." He hesitated just a moment, pulled by the responsibility of his job and at the same time by the time he had just spent with Rachel. "Do you want me to stop by this week and see how it's going?"

They both knew he didn't need to. Things seemed to be going quite well. But Gracie was a convenient excuse. For now.

"That would be nice," she said.

"I'll keep in touch." He turned and left. As he walked away, he couldn't help glancing over his shoulder, but Rachel was cleaning up and didn't look up.

The disappointment he felt surprised him.

"C'mon, honey. Hold still. I need to dry you off." Rachel lifted Gracie out of the bathtub and wrapped the squirming, wet girl in the towel. She tried not to rush things, but as had been the problem for the past week and a half, she was in a hurry and running behind.

She had finally gotten hold of LaReese on Tuesday and arranged a meeting for tonight. LaReese's reluctance to see her only made her more determined to keep this meeting. She had to take Gracie but knew that the child wasn't going to be sleeping much before nine tonight anyhow. Rachel had gotten caught up in one of her files and had let Gracie sleep too long this afternoon.

She knew part of her frustration lay with Eli. That moment in the park had been a turning point for her. When Eli had asked if she wanted him to stop by, she had found she couldn't say no.

She wanted him to come and yet was relieved he hadn't. The memories she'd shared with him of Keith gave her such mixed feelings. She hadn't spoken of Keith for a long time. Suddenly she felt afraid and vulnerable again. And yet, she had told Eli.

Gracie wriggled again and Rachel tried to catch her. The child whipped her head back and smacked Rachel directly on the lip. A flash of electric stars shot behind her eyes.

"You little stinker," she muttered, barely holding on to the toddler. Her eyes watered and her lip throbbed and, of course, right then the doorbell rang.

Rachel struggled to her feet, still holding Gracie, who seemed to realize what she had done and now lay quiescent in Rachel's arms, still wrapped in the towel. Rachel made her way down the long hallway, past her own room, then down the long flight of stairs to the front door. Though she was in a rush, she took her time on the carpeted steps. The last thing she needed was a broken leg like her mother.

The bell chimed again, echoing through the foyer as Rachel reached the landing. She wondered who would stop by at seven o'clock in the evening. It wasn't Pilar and Anne. They had come last night and lured Rachel away from her work, insisting that she take a break. She couldn't really afford it, but she also knew she needed the social interaction. Her life the past two weeks had consisted of juggling her care for Gracie and work. She had taken Sunday off, but that was three days ago and she was still paying for it. Working away from the office was hard. And it gave her less control.

"I'm coming, I'm coming," Rachel muttered, still on the stairs.

When she reached the bottom the marble floor was cool under her bare feet and she wrapped the towel tighter around Gracie. All she could see behind the frosted glass of the door was an indistinct figure backlit by the evening sun.

Her heart stuttered and she felt her breath hitch in her throat.

Since Sunday she had thought he might stop by again. But three days had gone by and she had decided that she'd read far more into her reactions to him than was there.

And now, here he was.

Chapter Ten

She clutched Gracie and slowly opened the door.

Eli stood on the step, tapping his motorcycle helmet against his leg, just as he had the football on Sunday afternoon. And just as he did then, tonight he wore blue jeans, a leather motorcycle jacket and an enigmatic smile. He looked up as the door opened, and his crooked smile drew out an answering one from her.

"Hey there," he said, his husky voice creating a faint ripple somewhere in the region of her stomach.

She tried to brush the feeling aside. Tried to act casual as she invited him in. This was sheer silliness. He was Gracie's doctor. He was just interested in Gracie's well-being. That was why he had stopped by.

But as she looked up into Eli's warm green eyes, common sense was brushed aside. She realized she hadn't felt lonely until now.

"Just finished the bath?" he said, tugging lightly on Gracie's damp curl.

"Eli here," Gracie crowed, wriggling with pleasure.

"Just getting ready to go out," she replied, shifting Gracie's weight to her hip.

Eli frowned. "This time of night?"

"Gracie had a long nap this afternoon," Rachel protested, feeling as if she suddenly had to justify her actions. "She's probably not going to sleep until at least nine o'clock. I need to go see a lady and I thought I could easily take Gracie along."

Eli raised one hand as if in surrender. "It's okay, Rachel. I'm not making a commentary on your mothering skills." He tilted her a crooked grin, a faint dimple winking at her from one corner of his mouth. "I was just hoping I could…" He paused, then shrugged, growing serious. "But you got things to do."

"I was just going to LaReese Binet's. A quick visit." Rachel hitched Gracie up, licking her sore lip. "You could come…if you want?"

Listen to us, Rachel thought. *Like a couple of teenagers trying to figure out if we like each other.* "I have a few ideas I want to run past LaReese. You could help."

"Me?" Eli pointed to himself and laughed.

"Why not? I hear that you have a great bedside manner…"

"With little *kids*…"

"And with this woman I need all the charm I can get."

"Charm?"

"Yeah."

He laughed, looked away as if considering, then back at her again. "Okay, Rachel. I'll come and see what I can do for you."

An unexpected feeling of pleasure spiraled up at his consent. "Okay. I've just got to get this girl dressed, put on some makeup, and then we can go." She smiled, and then winced as pain from her lip blossomed.

Eli frowned at her, and then bent closer. He lightly touched her now-swelling lip. His finger was cool and it sent a shiver down her spine.

"What happened?"

"Gracie has a very hard head." She tried to sound more casual then she felt, hoping he wouldn't notice the faint flush his gesture had created.

"Did you put a cold compress on it to take the swelling down?"

"It happened just before you came." She shrugged his concern away. "It will be okay. It's not like I'm going to be kissing anyone."

And didn't that sound provocative, she thought, the flush on her cheeks growing. "You can wait for us in the living room." She gestured to the large room off the foyer. "I'll just get Gracie dressed and then I'll be ready."

She turned away and almost ran back up the stairs, her bare feet making barely a sound in the pile carpeting.

She was being silly, she thought as she finished drying Gracie, who was babbling about Eli and Rachel and going out, her pleasure an enthusiastic counterpoint to the attraction that Rachel was hard pressed to deny.

She quickly dressed Gracie in a white shirt and pink coveralls, pulled her curls up in a ponytail and tied it with a perky bow. Gracie was fun to dress up, and certainly her mother had enough clothes for her.

"Okay, Gracie. I have to get ready now," she said, plunking the child on the counter to watch. "Don't fall off or I'll be in trouble with your pediatrician." She tucked her into the corner by the wall and gave her some bathtub toys to play with.

Her fingers were trembling slightly as she applied her makeup. "This is not a date," she muttered, swiping mascara over her already dark lashes. She wrinkled her nose at her reflection, and then smoothed the lipstick that Pilar had chosen for her over her lips.

Her hair, she couldn't do much about. She didn't have time to pin it up and decided to simply let it loose. Not her usual style by any means, but these days "usual" simply meant neat and clean. Neat and *professional* would have to wait until her mother was mobile again and Rachel had her life back.

She ran a brush through her hair, then pressed a hand to her stomach to still the silly flip-flopping that had started at the thought of spending the evening with Eli.

She took a long, slow breath and looked at herself in the mirror. "So he's good looking. And good with Gracie. And fun. And has a cute smile." She tried to diffuse the effect of his attributes by acknowledging them. "You can't afford to go there. It is too dangerous to get attached," she reminded herself. "Dangerous and foolhardy."

But as she carried Gracie down the stairs, the whimsical feelings that Eli had generated in her lately overcame her warnings.

She found Eli in front of a painting that hung above the marble fireplace. He turned as she came into the room.

"Is this you with your parents?" he asked, gesturing at the large portrait.

Rachel nodded, slightly embarrassed. The painting was ages old. She'd been five, sitting on her mother's lap, wearing a froufrou dress. Her parents hadn't hit their unconventional stage of their life, so her father wore a suit and ascot, and her mother, an evening gown and pearls.

"I have begged them time and time again to take it down or at least replace it with something less pretentious." She set Gracie on the floor. The toddler was heavy.

"Your parents are hardly pretentious," Eli said.

"No. Or conventional. Something I believe they learned hobnobbing with the rich and famous of New England. That painting was commissioned when we lived up there on the advice of my father's parents. My parents keep it up as a reminder."

"Of what?"

"Something they learned when they became Christians. That their money is a responsibility, not a right." Rachel glanced around the room at the furniture that her parents had collected over the years. Some of it was antique, handed down to Charles by his family. Other pieces were whimsical, gathered because they were comfortable and fun.

"And all these other people?" Eli gestured toward the many portraits that graced the walls.

"My father's family. The Nobles have a long and illustrious history," Rachel said, glancing at the portraits that portrayed her relatives through time.

"American nobility," Eli said quietly.

Rachel frowned at him. "Where did you hear that?"

"An article I read a while ago. When I first met your parents, I stumbled on it."

Rachel frowned at that. She didn't like to think that people were talking about them like that. "Well, as far as I'm concerned, nobility is earned, not bought."

"Eli carry me." Gracie toddled over to Eli's side and

banged her hands on his legs. He grinned down at her and picked her up.

"I hate to be pushy, but I should get going," Rachel said. "You can either follow me on your motorcycle, or come with me in my car."

"I'll come in the car, if it's okay with you."

It was more than okay. Since the afternoon in the park, he had occupied far too many of her thoughts. She had given him a part of herself that she hadn't shown many people. She still wasn't sure what had prompted the confession about Keith. Church maybe. Feeling vulnerable and maybe even a bit lonely. But Eli kept to ordinary topics of conversation as they drove. He quizzed her on what she hoped to accomplish with the meeting.

"She's been really skittish lately," Rachel explained. "Hesitant to commit her money. And it is a substantial amount. I'm afraid that she's been—" Rachel stopped, unwilling to say anything more to this man to whom she had already told so much.

"She's been what?"

"I'm sorry. I can't say."

"But it bothers you."

Rachel worried her lip, then winced as she bit the spot Gracie had hit. "It's complicated and I really don't know what to think." She glanced at Eli, who lounged back in his seat, his eyes on her as she drove. For a moment she longed to tell someone about her troubles at the Foundation. She should have been able to confide in Reuben, but he was the one she had concerns about.

Last night she had finally contacted him. When she asked him why he hadn't returned her calls, he said he had forgotten his cell phone.

He also said he didn't have time to bring over the information he had gotten on the charitable organization that he was researching for LaReese, said he had something else he was looking into. She wanted to believe him, but she couldn't.

And when she had connected to her computer at the Foundation this afternoon, she'd noticed that someone else had logged on to the office computer. Someone knew her password.

She let out a sigh, reluctant to tell Eli, yet needing to talk to someone. When Anita still worked for the Foundation, Rachel would confide in her. Lorna simply didn't inspire the same trust.

"Is there someone you can talk to?" Eli asked.

Rachel pulled into the visitor parking stall of LaReese's condo, parked the car and turned to Eli, pleased at the concern in his voice. "I would normally talk to my father about this, but he's too busy with Mom and I don't want to bother him."

"How about the board of the Foundation?"

Rachel shook her head. "No. This is internal. I need to find a way to deal with it on my own."

"You don't have to do everything on your own," Eli said.

Rachel didn't reply as she got out of the car, slipping the strap of her briefcase over her shoulder. "Lately, it seems like I do everything on my own," she said with a light laugh.

Eli was already unbuckling Gracie by the time Rachel came around to her side of the car. He handed Rachel the diaper bag, and shut the door.

They looked just like a little family, Rachel thought as they walked up the stairs to the entrance of LaReese's town house. Dad holding the baby, Mom holding the diaper bag. As she pushed the bell for LaReese's apartment she let the fleeting thought settle for a moment.

What would it be like to be married? To have a family?

She pulled herself up short, stopping the direction of her thoughts. Marriage was a word she hadn't used since Keith.

The memory of his name made her feel a touch of regret, followed by a niggle of disloyalty. Keith was the only one she had woven such daydreams around. There hadn't been anyone else before, or after.

Gracie was babbling to herself in a singsong voice that only added to the tension Rachel felt. She should have left her at home.

With whom? Eli?

Rachel was about to ring the bell again, when the door opened as if by itself. Rachel walked into a large entrance and was immediately greeted by a woman wearing a crisp blue dress. "Ms. Binet is waiting for you on the deck at the back." She turned and led them through another door, then across another open expanse that looked like a living room, to large French doors.

She leaned closer to Eli and whispered. "Don't let Gracie get away on you. I'm seeing visions of sticky handprints dancing all over the glass."

Eli chuckled as they were led out onto a large curved deck that was bordered by a stone handrail. Beyond the deck was a profusion of flowers, surrounded on two sides by a brick wall. The end of the garden overlooked the lush green of Winchester Park. LaReese had been sitting at a glass table shaded by a large umbrella and got up to greet them.

"Hello, Rachel, welcome again," she said with a polite smile for Rachel and an obviously brighter one for Gracie. Or maybe it was Eli.

"And I see you brought a friend," she simpered, batting her lashes.

It was definitely Eli.

"Eli Cavanaugh is Gracie's pediatrician. I have been taking care of my sister Gracie since our mother fell and broke her leg ten days ago." Rachel turned to Eli and made the proper introductions. Gracie cuddled closer to Eli when LaReese tried to talk to her, but Rachel was relieved to see that the child gave the older woman a bright smile anyway.

"What an adorable child. I had heard that your parents adopted a little girl. She has cerebral palsy, doesn't she?"

"Yes, she does," Rachel said.

"I thought they had lost their minds, adopting a special needs baby, but I can see why they were smitten with her in spite of her handicap." LaReese indicated the chairs across the table from her. "Sit down. Can I get you anything? Coffee? Sweet tea? Some juice for the little girl?"

"I'll have a sweet tea and Gracie would enjoy some apple or orange juice if you have it," Rachel said as she sat down. Eli declined both. LaReese made a barely perceptible motion to the woman behind her, who gave a curt nod and then left.

I need one of those, thought Rachel, fighting the urge to unzip her briefcase and get down to business. *A wonderful person who anticipates my needs, then fulfills them.* She smiled at LaReese, and asked after her health and how her nephew was doing in his new business venture. They chatted until the nameless woman returned with their refreshments.

Rachel was about to take Gracie from Eli, but he shook his head and gave her the apple juice himself. She smiled her thanks, and then looked back at LaReese, who had been watching them with a gentle smile on her face.

Rachel felt a flush creep up her neck, realizing how the situation must look to her. But she was here for business. She took a quick sip of her tea, then dove into her briefcase for the papers she had taken along.

"Rachel said your name is Cavanaugh. Is your family from here?" LaReese was asking Eli.

"My adoptive parents used to live here, Peggy and Tyrone Cavanaugh. My adoptive brother, Ben, still does," Eli said, setting Gracie's cup down on the table. He wiped her mouth with a napkin, looking like a seasoned father.

"You said adoptive. You weren't born a Cavanaugh?"

Eli shook his head. "No. My biological parents' names were Fulton. Darlene and Zeke Fulton."

LaReese thought for a moment, then shook her head. "Never heard of either family. How did you get adopted, then?"

"My brother, Ben, and I were both adopted through the Tiny Blessings agency."

LaReese glanced at Rachel. "Your parents used Tiny Blessings, didn't they? To adopt the girl?"

"Gracie was adopted through the agency, as well," Rachel agreed, giving "the girl" a name.

LaReese sat back, absently playing with her earrings. Her various rings glowed in the lowering sunlight as she looked past them to the park.

"Barnaby Harcourt started that agency, didn't he?" LaReese asked with a light frown.

"He was founder and director until he died." Rachel had

known Barnaby through her work at the Foundation, but had never been comfortable around him. He had a barely definable air of greed that always made Rachel feel uneasy. She enjoyed working with Kelly Young, the current director, much better.

"Dale and I talked about adopting at one time but Dale was uneasy about it," LaReese said quietly. A sad expression twisted her face. "We didn't have any children of our own. Not now, anyway."

Rachel picked up the vague reference and stilled her own restlessness. "Did you have a child once?"

LaReese nodded, her eyes drifting past Rachel as if to another time. "He was only three years old. Just a little older than this one," she said, angling her chin at Gracie.

"What happened?" Rachel asked, pitching her voice low, encouraging LaReese's trust.

LaReese pressed her lips together as if holding back her sorrow. "It was a long time ago. A long time." She looked over at Rachel with a sad smile. "He had some unpronounceable illness, very rare. He died. The doctor said our chances were one in two that we would have another child with the same disease. So we decided not to have any more. I could not put myself through that again."

"I understand," Rachel said. And she did. She could see in LaReese's eyes an echo of her own pain. Of her own decision. Better to keep yourself free from attachments than to face the chance of that pain again.

But even as she thought that, she was fully aware of Eli sitting beside her. Eli who, lately, had been occupying more and more of her thoughts. Eli, who brought out emotions in her that she had tried to fight.

"I think it was a mistake, though," LaReese continued,

twisting a ring around her finger. "I think we should have tried again. Loving someone is always a chance. You open yourself up to the possibility of losing them. But the pleasure, the joy that comes with it is worth the potential of pain." She glanced at Gracie, and Rachel's eyes followed her gaze. Only her gaze was caught by Eli's. He was watching her with an enigmatic smile on his face. Again she felt that connection. A yearning. And her heart went all quivery with the idea that maybe, just maybe…

"Anyway, that is in the past," LaReese said, placing her hands on the table, her rings thunking on the glass. "I'm sure you didn't come here to discuss that." She looked back at Rachel, all business now. "I have to confess I'm a little confused as to what the Foundation has been doing for me. Or trying to do for me," she said primly. "You are here today. Last week it was that young person from your office with another man. I am not sure who I am supposed to be dealing with."

Rachel suddenly stilled at LaReese's words. She carefully banked her anger with Reuben. She had distinctly told him that she would deal with LaReese personally. "What did he tell you?"

LaReese frowned at her. "Oh, it was the young lady that did all the talking. Something about an organization that brings Christmas gifts to children of people in jail. I like the idea that these children are taken care of."

"There are some very good organizations that do this kind of work," Rachel said carefully, sensing the hesitancy in LaReese, as well. "Some more prominent than others. Do you remember the name?"

LaReese gave it to her and Rachel felt a cold chill travel down her spine. She had heard of this group all right, a scam from the word go. If Reuben was pushing LaReese to give money to this group, then it only stood to reason that he would gain from it, as well. No wonder he had been so elusive lately. "This group was never vetted by me," she said, her anger growing.

"What do you mean?" LaReese looked genuinely puzzled now.

"We do an extensive background search on any and all nonprofit organizations that apply to us for funding or for assistance with their fund-raising. We make sure they are on the up-and-up and that they do not charge extensive administration costs. There are some nonprofit organizations out there who charge up to eighty percent administration costs, leaving very little to the actual group they are supposed to be taking care of." Rachel caught herself, forced herself to slow down. She tended to get quite emotional where some of the more sleazy operations were concerned. And knowing that Reuben was involved made it even worse. "Please tell me you didn't sign anything with them."

"I didn't. I wanted to talk to you."

Rachel felt herself go slack with relief. "I'm glad you did. I want you to know that I would never recommend any organization to you that I have not personally vetted. And this one is just a huge money pit. I can't believe Reuben did this."

LaReese frowned. "Reuben was the young man with you the last time you came here, wasn't he?"

"Yes."

"Well, this wasn't Reuben. This was someone named Lorna."

Chapter Eleven

Rachel sat back in stunned surprise. "Lorna? Lorna Kirkpatrick?"

LaReese nodded, clearly confused. "She works for you, doesn't she?"

"She's my assistant." *Or maybe "was."* Rachel took in a long breath and rubbed the tips of her fingers over her temples. She felt cold inside as little things suddenly came together. How Lorna had shifted Rachel's suspicions to Reuben. The other day, when she could see that someone had tried to get into her computer, Reuben had been gone that day. The only person around was Lorna.

How could she have done this? Rachel had trusted her, had believed her over Reuben. She leaned back against her chair, feeling slightly nauseated at the thought of Lorna's betrayal.

She glanced at Eli. Gracie still sat contentedly on his lap, but his attention was on Rachel, a frown of concern on his face. She gave him a careful smile, then turned back to LaReese, struggling to pull herself together. In the past few minutes her perceptions and trusts had been twisted and rearranged. It was difficult to orient herself, but she had to. This was her job. LaReese was her focus.

She gave LaReese a smile that held more confidence than Rachel felt. But she knew one thing from moving in the circles of the wealthy. Confidence bred confidence. If she wanted LaReese on board, she had to project emotions she wasn't feeling right now.

It would be easier to do it in her usual suit, with her hair worn up, rather than the soft t-shirt and khaki pants she had slipped on.

"Okay, there's no harm done so far." At least, not where LaReese was concerned. Rachel kept her tone brisk to cover her hurt at Lorna's deception. "I am so thankful you didn't do anything rash."

"Well, to tell you the truth, the project wasn't something I was really excited about. I like the idea of doing something with children." She looked over at Gracie, who was scribbling with Eli's pen on a napkin. "I don't mind the idea of Tiny Blessings, though I never did like that snake who founded it, Barnaby Harcourt." She sniffed, then, as an afterthought, added, "Bless his departed soul."

Her comment about the late Mr. Harcourt made Rachel think of LaReese's story of her son. And in that moment, Rachel knew that her own instincts about what would interest LaReese had been right.

"Tiny Blessings is a good cause, as well. But I don't think it is as good a match as what I had in mind. I would like you to think of the pediatric ward of the Richmond hospital," Rachel said, gently pushing a brochure across the table to LaReese. And in the slight narrowing of La-

Reese's eyes and the way she started to lean forward, Rachel caught the beginnings of interest.

Gracie was growing restless and Rachel glanced at her as LaReese perused the brochure Rachel had brought along.

Eli got up, bent over Rachel and said quietly, "I'll just let her walk in the yard for a bit."

His breath was warm against her ear, intimate. Rachel angled her head just so, and his face was only inches from hers. She could see the soft green of his eyes, how the sun gilded his eyelashes.

She swallowed, then nodded, and felt a faint tingle all the way down to her toes when his smile crinkled his cheeks.

"Do you mind, Ms. Binet?" Eli asked, his head still close to Rachel's.

LaReese's maternal expression made Rachel even more self-conscious about Eli's presence. "Of course not, Dr. Cavanaugh. You go ahead."

As Eli left with Gracie toddling unevenly alongside him, LaReese's smile faded away.

"That poor little girl," LaReese said. "What kind of life will she have?"

Rachel heard an echo of her own concern for Gracie in LaReese's voice, and she glanced back over her shoulder at Eli, who towered over the toddler, projecting protectiveness and strength. "I think she will have a life as full and rich as she wants," Rachel said quietly. "She has a whole team devoted to her care and support." Rachel turned back to LaReese, seeing another opportunity to encourage her giving. "The hospital has a variety of clinics that she attends that will help her with her walking and, later on, with other life skills. She is a bright, intelligent child. She has people who love her and help her along the way."

"Like you and Dr. Cavanaugh."

Rachel almost blushed at the linking of their names, but she carried on. "And, more importantly, my parents." Rachel turned back to the brochure. "I know that giving to the hospital isn't as romantic and exciting as an individual cause is, but I want to let you know what your money can do."

But even as Rachel explained to LaReese how her donation would be used, she found she had to work extra hard to maintain her focus on her client.

And not on the appealing man walking in the garden with her little sister.

Rachel set Gracie's diaper bag on the change table of her darkened room while Eli gently laid the little girl in her bed. He pulled the quilt around Gracie and tucked her in, then smoothed a stray curl back from her head.

Rachel felt a peculiar sensation in her midsection at the sight of the tall man being so gentle with Gracie. He would make a wonderful father.

The errant thought hovered a moment, making her wonder what his children would look like.

She followed him out through the hallway and down the stairs to the front entrance, where his motorcycle helmet still sat on the floor. The restlessness she had felt all evening would not be stilled even though she had accomplished something important with LaReese. She wanted to blame her edginess on her discovery of Lorna's disloyalty, but she knew that was only a small part.

A larger part consisted of her changing feelings toward

this handsome and kind man who carried himself with such self-assurance. Who had a gentle strength that called to her.

Now, she didn't want him to leave yet. She wanted to find out more about him. What he liked to do. What his childhood was like. What made him happy, sad.

"By the way, thanks so much for coming along," Rachel said as he bent over to retrieve his helmet.

He gave her a crooked smile. "Someone had to baby-sit."

She laughed at that. "Gracie is pretty relaxed around you."

"And you seem more relaxed around her."

"As long as she stays healthy, I feel like I have a handle on her care." She gave a short laugh. "One of the few things it seems I have a handle on lately."

"I'm guessing you're talking about your assistant."

Rachel felt again a low pull of embarrassment that her employee's defection had been unveiled in front of him. Bad enough that LaReese had to be the one to let her know. That Eli had to see how poor a judge of character she was somehow hurt even more. "I feel…violated." She hugged herself, as if warding off the inevitable problems she would have to face tomorrow.

Eli took a step closer and laid his hand on her shoulder. "It's not your fault. She obviously knew what she was doing."

"And she was very good at it," Rachel said with a sigh. "When I think of the information she could have gotten her hands on…" She shuddered, thankful for Eli's support. "Trouble was, she had such good credentials. I can't believe I was that blind. I feel so…unprofessional."

Eli curved his fingers around her shoulder, his fingers warm through the material of her shirt. "You did good tonight, though. You knew better than Lorna what LaReese wanted." He gave her shoulder a gentle squeeze. "And thanks to you, I might be able to pick out some shiny new equipment."

In spite of her frustration, Rachel had to laugh.

"I am pleased that LaReese finally settled on a cause I know will be close to her heart."

"So you can take it easy for a while?"

"I wish. Now I have to find another assistant—after I fire Lorna. I've never had to do that before."

"I don't suppose you could subcontract that job out?" Eli said, his faint humor making her smile again.

"No. This one I have to do on my own. I just hope she hasn't done any other damage." She bit her lip, then winced as again she hit the spot Gracie had banged with her head.

Eli frowned, then touched her lip with his finger. "This looks a little swollen yet."

Rachel's heart stuttered at his touch. "No," she said, strangely short of breath. "It feels fine."

"Good." He shifted his weight, bringing him closer to her. As if it had a life of its own, her hand came up to rest on his shoulder. His face blurred and then his lips were on hers. Warm, gentle, inviting.

Rachel's eyes drifted closed. And as she returned his kiss she felt a momentary panic, which almost caused her to pull away—until his arms slipped around her, held her close.

And for the first time in years, Rachel felt curiously whole. She leaned into his embrace, allowing herself to be supported.

Eli was the first to pull away, though he kept his arms around her.

He traced the line of her features with his fingers, as if reading Braille, his mouth lifted in that bemused smile that she had come to associate with him. Rachel slowly steadied herself, drew back, her hand resting on his chest. This felt good, right.

"Is this ethical?" She could barely get the words past the sudden constriction in her throat. But she needed to lighten the suddenly heavy atmosphere. To step back from the very place she had avoided falling into for so many years. "Kissing my sister's pediatrician?"

She felt the rumble of his chuckle under her fingers. He smoothed a strand of hair away from her face, then stepped back as if giving them both some much-needed distance.

"I don't think you're going to report me and I doubt Gracie will lodge a complaint."

She lowered her gaze, drew her hand away, retreating as the full implications of what they had just done registered. As long as she had denied her attraction to him, as long as she had kept herself apart from him, had been able to deal with these new and unwelcome emotions.

But now?

She had gotten a taste of something she had missed for so very long. She didn't even know it until his lips had touched hers. Until she had surrendered her will, her emotions, her feelings to this man.

When she'd walked away from Keith's grave site, devastated by her loss, she had vowed she would never allow herself to be in such a vulnerable position again. To allow herself to care for someone so deeply was to open herself up to the possibility of pain. It had taken her years to regain her equilibrium, to forget how devastated she had been when she had to face her life alone again.

But now?

"I—I shouldn't have done that," she stammered, wrenching her gaze away from his. "I'm sorry."

"I'm not. And I know what you're thinking, Rachel." He tipped her chin up, forcing her to look up at him. "I think you're scared."

His very perception created a connection she had not felt with any man since Keith. That he knew and understood seemed to give her a solid footing from which to consider him.

"I am."

He caressed her chin with his thumb. "That's okay. I'm a little scared, too. But we have time. Lots of time."

She sighed lightly, then smiled. "We." In spite of her fear, she liked the sound of that.

He brushed a kiss over the top of her head, then, with a whispered "Bye, Rachel," he left.

Rachel closed the door behind him, listening for the sound of his motorcycle going down the driveway. She leaned her head against the cool leaded glass, and felt a sudden need to pray.

"Watch over him, Lord," she said quietly. "Please don't let anything happen to him." A familiar shaft of dread pierced her, shaking her to her core. Did she really dare do this again? Open herself up to someone else? Risk the pain of loss?

Gracie's muffled cry filtered down the stairs and she pushed herself away from the glass. As she ran up the stairs to attend to her sister, she realized with a sinking feeling that she already had.

* * *

Eli tapped the button on the remote, surfing through the channels. Nothing caught his eye. Nothing caught his fancy. Though he was sitting on his own couch in his own house, his mind was firmly on the woman he had left behind over an hour ago.

The woman he had kissed over an hour ago.

What had prompted such an impulsive move?

Restless, he got up from the couch and walked up to the room he was currently sleeping in. Ben was supposed to come by and help him finish the master bedroom in a couple of days. If things went as he planned, his house would be completed in six months. The next step of the master plan was a new car. And then landscaping.

And then, according to the list, he was supposed to be building up his investment portfolio, and then, maybe then, looking at finding someone to share his neat, tidy and orderly life with.

The plan had seemed sound when he first drew it up. But that was before Rachel.

Eli pulled open the bottom drawer of his dresser and yanked out the box of photos he had taken from Peggy and Tyrone Cavanaugh's place. He thought once again of what Rachel had suggested to him. That maybe the Cavanaughs had good reasons for keeping the pictures away from him.

He flipped through them, trying to find traces of himself in his parents' faces. He thought he caught a glimpse of his chin in his mother's, his eyes in his father's. Or maybe it was just wishful thinking.

He was adult enough to realize that it was the Cavanaughs who were his real parents, but at the same time, like many adopted children, he still had a desire to learn what he could about his own parents. His file at Tiny Blessings had held precious little information and any searching he had done had met dead ends.

So why did he care?

His mind, like a homing beacon, drifted back to Rachel again. He glanced around the house and wondered what she would think of it. He smiled at the direction of his thoughts. Wondered if his plan was slowly being worn away by a pair of hazel eyes.

Rachel stared with disbelief at the alarm clock. She had been tossing and turning for only an hour. It seemed like forever. Over and over she replayed the scene with Eli, felt again the touch of his lips on hers. Like a skip on a DVD, it played over and over again.

Each time it was as if a new emotion caught her. Elation fought with fear, which was replaced with confusion. For so long she had held her heart whole and to herself, she didn't know how to let go of it, didn't dare.

Her mind slipped back to the church service Sunday, how Reverend Fraser had encouraged them to let God take control of their lives.

She pushed herself out of bed, snapped on her bedside lamp, pulled a robe around herself and padded down to her father's office. Papers were strewn over the desk in a completely un-Rachel-like fashion. She ignored it and walked to the shelves where she knew her father kept his religious books, and found a Bible.

She pulled it off the shelf and brought it back upstairs. Her parents had their own Bible by their bedside. This was a hardcover given to them the day of their wedding.

She slipped back into bed and started reading randomly.

A piece of paper marked a page, so she turned to it. It was the book of Second Corinthians, chapter twelve. An underlined verse caught her eye. "But He said to me 'My grace is sufficient for you, for My power is made perfect in weakness….'" She stopped there and read it again. Power made perfect in weakness? Further on she read, "For when I am weak, then I am strong."

How could weakness be strength?

And again Rachel felt as if her perspective had spun around. She knew the verse and had heard it used in sermons. But now, during this time when she felt the least in control of her life, to read this was like a gentle push in another direction. Another way of looking at strength and weakness.

And letting go.

She considered the day she'd brought Grace to the gait clinic at the hospital—how her weakness hadn't held her back. How she had relied on other people with a simple trust. Her dependence on other people gave her a strength she could not have on her own. The thought gave Rachel pause.

"How's Mom doing?" Rachel curled up in the deep cushions of her favorite couch, the phone tucked under one ear. As she listened to her father she flipped through the papers of the file on her lap.

Another application to the Foundation. She was thankful this one was for a consultation on a donation. Something she hadn't had for a while. Not since Lorna had started.

This morning she had made a special trip to the Foundation office to tell Lorna to her face that she was fired. It had been difficult to do, but while she cleaned up Lorna's desk, she discovered that Lorna had lured away other donors while in the Foundation's employ. She still felt the sting of Lorna's betrayal, but even worse than that, she felt the heaviness of the workload.

She needed two more pairs of hands, eyes and ears if she was going to get done what she needed to. She stifled a yawn. Last night she had stayed awake longer than usual, reading through the Bible. Searching for comfort, for strength.

"Beatrice is very determined and the doctors are very pleased with her progress," Charles was saying. "But she misses Gracie desperately. I don't suppose there's any way you could get her here to visit?"

Rachel closed her eyes, pinching the bridge of her nose. "Sorry, Dad, I am just swamped here."

"Couldn't you give some of your work over to those capable assistants you just hired?"

She hadn't told him about Lorna yet. He didn't need any more burdens on his shoulders right now. "'Just' being the operative word, Dad," she said. "When did the doctors say Mom was able to come back?"

"They've revised the estimate. They figure now it should be in at least three weeks. Could I possibly talk to Gracie?"

"Sorry, Dad. She's in bed now. She had a busy day." Rachel had had to take Gracie to her office at the Foundation to clear up after Lorna was escorted out, and then to a visit to the hospital for yet another clinic. She was grateful that Gracie's sunny disposition had been on display until they came home. But then Rachel was treated to the dark side of her sister. Gracie was cranky, irritable and wouldn't eat.

After her bath, Rachel put her in bed and the little girl was asleep in seconds. Which made Rachel feel even more guilty for dragging the poor child around.

She talked to her father for a few more minutes, her own work nagging at her even while she spoke. Charles seemed to sense her distraction and said goodbye.

No sooner had he hung up than the phone rang again.

Rachel sighed and hit the button without bothering to check who was calling. "Rachel here."

"Hey there. How are you?"

Eli's deep voice washed over her, smoothing away her irritation. Rachel sank back against the soft cushions. She had hoped to see Eli this afternoon, but all she got was a glimpse of him striding down the hallway with an entourage of interns. Enough of a glimpse to kick her heart rate up a notch.

"Just finished talking to Dad," she said. "Mom's doing good. But she won't be home for three weeks yet."

"Sorry I missed you at the clinic. I found out about the clinic the same time we had an emergency."

"Everything okay?"

"Now it is."

He sounded tired, too. "So what are you doing tonight?" she asked.

"As little as possible. I had hoped to get some work done on the house, but that isn't going to happen soon."

She asked about his house, he asked about her work. Their words danced along the edges of their feelings. The kiss wasn't mentioned, though the memory of it was a palpable presence. They talked about movies. Books. Safe, easy topics.

"How are the plans for the picnic coming?" he asked.

"Good. Busy. Wondering if I can do it all," she said.

"I've already heard mention of it among the higher-ups. It sounds like it's a pretty big deal."

"It's supposed to be casual, but casual creates its own peculiar problems." She hesitated for a moment. The picnic was a strictly "by invitation only" affair. Very exclusive.

And she wanted him there. "Would you like to come?" she asked.

Eli laughed. "I'll definitely feel out of place, from what I hear."

"Oh, c'mon. You seem comfortable enough around my parents."

"Your parents are special."

"I'll say," Rachel said with a laugh. Then she grew serious. "Please come. I'd love to see you there."

She winced at what she had just said. She sounded desperate.

"In that case," Eli said with a hint of a smile in his voice, "I suppose I could show up."

Rachel relaxed again. "That would be nice." She gave him the date, told him it was casual dress. He said he would see about getting the time off. They chatted some more, but then Rachel could hear that Eli had another call, and let him go.

When Rachel put the phone down, she felt as if she had come back to reality from a place of uncertainty. She had invited him to the picnic. It was a simple polite invitation, nothing more.

"You could give me some of the work for the picnic," Reuben said, from the deep leather chair of her father's study. It was early morning and he was taking notes on some files that Rachel had been working on.

"I hardly know where to start delegating," Rachel said with an exasperated sigh. "Besides, where would you find the time? I feel bad enough that you had to work this evening."

"I think I have more time than you do. My days aren't as busy as they could be." The tapping of his pen on the file relayed his impatience. "You look exhausted, Rachel. I know you're busy with your sister. Now you have to find someone else to do Lorna's job and train her, and I know you don't have the time. Let me take care of some of this stuff."

Rachel bit her lip, looking over the master file for the picnic she had pulled up on the computer. According to her list she had to verify some deliveries, confirm with the caterer and then arrange for extra help for the gardener. She knew exactly what she wanted, as she did every year. And every year the picnic was a huge success. Without being overly proud, she knew a lot of it had to do with her intervention. The picnic had been her brainchild and had become a premier event for the Foundation and a direct reflection on it. Much of the prestige the Foundation enjoyed was an indirect result of contacts made at the picnic. To let go of it now…

The tapping of Reuben's pen increased. "Rachel, I think we need to talk."

The words drew her attention. When men, who weren't the "talking" types, made this proclamation, it usually meant something serious was coming down. "What's on your mind, Reuben?" she asked, a feeling of dread pushing at her.

"Control. Job opportunities." He shoved his hand through his hair and got up from the chair. "When I started this job, it was with the idea that I would slowly be taking over more responsibility. That I would be going somewhere."

"You've only been with the Foundation three months…"

"And in those three months, I have to confess I haven't learned a whole lot. You do it all. In fact, there are times I think you do too much. I know I have a ways to go, but I am also starting to realize that I can see an end to this job. I'm young enough, but I know that I am not going to waste my time in a dead-end job. I don't think it's wrong to be ambitious, so that means I also have to be realistic."

Rachel blinked. His words were a direct echo of Anita's when she quit. She, too, had spoken of dead ends in the job. Panic clawed at her. She couldn't afford to lose Reuben. Not now. But what else could she do? The Foundation had gotten to its current position thanks to her work.

She looked at Reuben, wishing she knew what to say.

"For when I am weak, then I am strong." The words drifted into her consciousness, featherlight, yet they caught her attention.

"I should let you know that I've also been talking to Anita about this job." Reuben's gaze slid away. "It may sound like we were talking behind your back, and I mean no disrespect, but she said the same thing. In fact, she might not have quit if she had been given more responsibility."

Rachel felt the words like a blow. Anita would have stayed?

She closed her eyes and pictured her fingers releasing

their grip on what she thought she needed to hold on to. Had she been so controlling? But if she hadn't taken charge of the company, what would have happened?

"Please, Rachel. I'm sorry. I shouldn't have said anything." Reuben sounded truly distressed.

Rachel looked up at him as her thoughts reassembled. And as his words echoed through her mind, she realized he was right. She drew a deep breath and then took a chance.

"Okay. I do have an important job for you. Find a capable replacement for Lorna and I'll put you in charge of the caterer for the picnic." She pulled the pages out of the computer, glanced at them, then, before she could change her mind, she handed them to him. "This is a list that I usually go over. If you have any questions…"

Reuben grinned and flipped through them. "Okay. We'll start simple."

Rebecca almost laughed. "Finding a replacement for Lorna doesn't seem simple to me."

He gave her a cheeky wink. "I've got that covered already. I'm going to give Anita a call. Let her know that you are now into delegating."

Rachel almost laughed at his brash statement. "If you can get Anita to come back to work for me, then you deserve all the delegating I can pass off."

Two hours later, Reuben left the house whistling. Rachel watched him jog down the brick sidewalk to his car and get in. She could see from the grin on his face that he was well pleased with himself.

Had she done the right thing? Was he overconfident in his ability? A little too bold?

Rachel pushed her second thoughts aside. She had chosen him from a number of applicants precisely for the qualities she was now questioning. He would do just fine. She had to trust him.

She had to trust, period.

Chapter Twelve

"Are you sure you don't need anything?" Rachel asked Reuben for about the fourth time. A faint breeze caught her hair and tugged a few wisps loose. She was glad the sun had come out just before the first guests arrived at the plantation for the annual Noble Foundation community picnic. And that the sun was not too warm. Rachel had fretted all morning about the weather, just as she had about the arrangements. And she had complete control over neither.

Reuben caught her by the shoulders and gave her a light shake. "I'm fine. Things are fine. Everyone is fine. Go and mingle and charm people so that when it comes time to ask for more money for Tiny Blessings, the Foundations coffers will overflow."

"Now, Reuben, we're going to pretend we never heard that word." Anita came up behind Reuben and smiled at Rachel. "Though everyone knows the reason for the picnic, it is considered ill-bred to even mention the word 'money.'"

Rachel grinned at her former secretary, who had of late become her new assistant. As promised, Reuben had managed to talk Anita into coming back with the promise of more responsibility. Thanks to Reuben and the reality of Gracie's needs, Rachel had slowly gotten used to the idea of delegating. To her surprise, she felt freer, lighter.

Gracie tugged on her hand again. "Are you sure?" Rachel had to ask just one more time.

Since the guests had arrived, she had been feeling disoriented. Usually she was doing what Anita and Reuben were now doing. Choreographing the movement of guests, supervising the food, making sure that everything flowed smoothly. The picnic was always touted as a casual affair, but even "casual" for the huge number of guests that always came, required a lot of behind-the-scenes direction.

Reuben squeezed her shoulders in reassurance. "Remember the magic words—'Delegate. Let go.' Repeat after me. 'Delegate. Let go.' Say it."

"Delegate. Let go," Rachel replied with a laugh. "I'm learning."

"Eli. Eli. You come," Gracie called out.

Rachel's heart jumped as she turned in time to see Eli bend over and scoop Gracie up in his arms. His sea-green eyes flicked over Reuben, then rested on Reuben's hands which were still holding Rachel.

Rachel tried not to blush and eased away from Reuben, hoping Eli would not read more into the situation than was there. "Eli, this is my assistant, Reuben and my…" She caught herself before she said "secretary," "…my other assistant, Anita. Eli is Gracie's doctor."

Who happened to kiss me the other night.

She shook the thought away, but when she glanced at

him, she could easily remember the feel of his mouth on hers. She blinked, then pulled her attention back to the introductions.

Eli shook Reuben's and Anita's hands, balancing Gracie who had looped one arm around his neck. "Nice to meet you."

"Eli. We have a huge favor to ask of you," Reuben said brightly. "Rachel is learning to delegate. She's not very good at it, but with a little practice, we are sure it will come. Would you be so kind as to take her around to all the people she is supposed to be circulating amongst and keep her away from us to whom she has delegated responsibility?"

Eli glanced at Rachel, his eyes lingering on her face. "I think I could manage that." Eli held out his arm like an old-fashioned gentleman and Rachel had no choice but to take it and walk away with him.

"I'm glad you could come," Rachel said when they were a safe distance away from Reuben and Anita. They had been studying Eli with too-avid interest.

"I traded a few favors," Eli said, tucking her arm closer to his. "You're not the only one that has to learn to delegate. To let go."

His comment made her look up at him with puzzlement. "What do you mean?"

The shifting leaves of the large trees overhead made the muted sunlight dance over the planes of his face as he smiled at her. Just as Eli was about to answer, Gracie's hands clutched Rachel's hair.

"You silly girl," Rachel said with a shaky laugh. "You pulled my hair loose."

Gracie just laughed and wiggled. "Go down," she demanded, and Eli complied.

"I should go to the house first and re-do my hair," Rachel said, trying to fix what Gracie had undone.

"Wear it loose," Eli said, plucking a pin from her hair. "It fits better with what you're wearing. After all, isn't casual the impression you are trying to achieve?"

Rachel glanced down at her pale green capris and sandals, topped with a cotton camisole. The outfit was casual compared to what she used to wear to work, and dressy compared to the clothes she'd been wearing recently.

Eli's crooked smile challenged her, so with a few quick tugs, she freed the rest of her hair. She slipped the pins in her pocket, then finger-combed her shoulder-length hair back from her face. "There. How does that look?"

"Looks great," Eli said.

Then, to her surprise, he reached out and fingered a strand of hair away from her face.

"I like it when you wear your hair down." His hand lingered, cupping her chin, and for a heart-stopping moment Rachel thought he was going to kiss her again.

And she wanted him to.

"We better go, before Gracie runs away," she said with a light laugh to cover her breathlessness.

They caught up to the child and each took her by one hand. They looked like a family, Rachel thought. Just as they had when they went to LaReese's place.

At that precise moment he turned and their gazes met. Neither looked away.

Everything else around them fell away. It was only her and Eli. His expression grew serious as he half turned to her. Then Gracie pulled on Rachel's hand, and the moment was broken.

As they walked, they passed a table that held an assortment of salads. One of the bowls was almost empty.

"Excuse me," she said to Eli, reluctantly letting go of Gracie's hand. "I have to take care of this."

Eli lifted Gracie up and caught her hand in his. "No, you don't. Reuben and Anita have it all under control."

Rachel frowned and was about to protest, when a woman carrying a large plastic-covered bowl brushed past her, and quickly replaced the salad.

"See?" Eli said with a lift of his eyebrows.

Rachel laughed in spite of herself. "Okay. I think I'm getting it." She drew in a deep breath, looked around, and realized that she could get used to this. The picnic was often a hurried, rushed affair for her as she juggled her social commitments while keeping things running smoothly.

She glanced at Eli, who was still smirking at her, and thought how nice it was to be able to simply visit with people. And to have Eli at her side as she did.

"I think it's going to be a wonderful day," Rachel said with a saucy smile.

"I hope so." Eli wove his fingers through hers.

Then together they walked toward Reverend John Fraser and his wife Naomi. Rachel made the necessary introductions, but as she chatted with them, her entire attention was on Eli.

The afternoon wore on. Eli had managed to pull Rachel aside to what he thought was a quiet spot to eat. But even then, people dropped by to talk to her. In the process he had gotten advice on what kind of Learjet he should buy if he was in the market, why he should be putting money into land around the Seattle area and why it was important to be on top of your investment portfolio.

Yes, he had his own plans, but to fit in with this crowd he would have to aim a little higher, work a little longer, expand the five-year plan to at least ten.

And with each conversation he felt as if a gulf grew between him and Rachel. He had a well-paying job, but he also had debts because of the training for that well-paying job. And the lifestyles he was faced with were so far removed from the simple life he had lived with Peggy and Tyrone Cavanaugh that he may as well be on another planet. Though he didn't doubt the sincerity of the people he met or their kindness, he just knew that this standard of living was not something he aspired to.

What he didn't know was, was it something Rachel expected?

"Are you okay?" Rachel was asking, as they found a place to get rid of their plates.

Had his dissatisfaction shown? He flashed a smile. "I'm fine. Just feeling a little overwhelmed."

"It is a lot of new faces to absorb," Rachel said, taking Gracie by the hand. "But in time you'll get to know them."

"Maybe."

Rachel was about to say something when someone else caught her attention.

"Mayor Morrow, Mrs. Morrow, how are you today?" she said, as an older couple came up to join them. "Enjoying the nice weather?"

Rachel's breezy attitude and encouraging smile elicited one from Lindsay Morrow, the mayor's wife. Eli wasn't surprised. Rachel seemed to charm even the most intractable person.

Rachel appeared more relaxed in these surroundings with these people than she had the first time they met. As he watched her smile, angle her head, lightly touch people, he saw a softer side of her.

"I'd like you to meet Dr. Cavanaugh," Rachel was saying, turning to Eli with a warm smile. "Eli, this is Mayor Morrow and his wife Lindsay."

Lindsay had that starved-to-perfection look that some older women seemed to think attractive. Instead it gave her a sharp, brittle look, which was re-emphasized by her severely tailored suit jacket and slacks.

"How nice to meet you, Dr. Cavanaugh," Lindsay said, holding out her hand. She held his a little longer than necessary, held his gaze a little too intently as if studying him. "I understand you were adopted by the Cavanaughs through Tiny Blessings."

Eli pulled his hand away as soon as he thought polite, wondering what she was up to. "Yes, I was. I was six years old when I joined their family."

"I see." Lindsay gave him a polite smile and suddenly looked uninterested.

"Quite a good turnout," Gerald Morrow was saying to Rachel, his eyes traveling over the gathering. "I notice that even the Harcourts have made an appearance."

"I was pleased to see them," Rachel said. "Their father had a hand in starting Tiny Blessings, after all."

"And this little one is your child?" Lindsay was asking, gesturing toward Gracie, who hung onto Eli's and Rachel's hands.

Rachel laughed. "No, this is my sister. Our parents adopted her from Tiny Blessings. I'm taking care of her while my mother recuperates from a fall. Dr. Cavanaugh is her pediatrician."

"A pediatrician. How interesting," Lindsay was saying, in a tone that seemed to imply what she thought of his chosen profession.

"It is, actually," Eli said easily, taking up the unspoken challenge to his line of work. "Children are one of the more challenging branches of medicine. But what I like the best about them is that they are completely honest."

Lindsay's eyes narrowed, and Eli realized that he might have said the wrong thing. He kept his smile in place. Lindsay Morrow may be the mayor's wife, but that didn't mean anything to him.

Gerald glanced down at Gracie. "So this child was adopted through Tiny Blessings." He nodded, looking suddenly thoughtful. "That is quite a step for your parents. To adopt a child they know nothing about." Lindsay bit her lip and looked away. Gerald patted her on the arm and gave them an apologetic look. "Lindsay and I could never have children. We had thought about adoption, but we were just not sure. You never know what kind of child you get when you adopt and you never seem to know enough about their parents."

Eli felt his face go tight at their implication. He glanced at Rachel, trying to gauge her reaction, but she was looking at Lindsay with sympathy.

"Adoption is not for everyone," she said diplomatically. Then she brightened and waved at a woman who was walking toward them. "Oh, I'm so glad. Sandra Lange came after all."

Mayor Morrow frowned and glanced at Lindsay, who was now clutching his arm, whispering in his ear. "If you'll excuse us, please, Rachel. My wife is not feeling well."

Rachel turned back to them. "I'm so sorry. You can take her into the house if you wish."

Lindsay shook her head. "Thank you, but I would prefer to go home." She started walking, pulling Gerald alongside her.

Eli thought she looked pretty energetic for someone who claimed to be ill. But then, what would he know. He was "just" a pediatrician. Though her inference made him smile, it still rankled to hear his profession slighted.

He followed Rachel to the woman who was watching Mayor Morrow and his wife as they left.

"Hello, Sandra," Rachel said with a smile, catching the woman's attention. "I am so glad you came. Sandra Lange, I would like you to meet Eli Cavanaugh."

Rachel tossed Eli a bright smile, which he couldn't help but return, then turned back to Sandra. Here was someone he could feel comfortable around. She looked delightfully ordinary and approachable in her blue jeans and T-shirt.

"How are you feeling?" Rachel asked, laying a hand on her shoulder.

"I'm good. We missed you girls the past couple of Sundays at the diner," Sandra was saying.

"I've been busy."

"I see that," Sandra said, giving Eli a knowing look.

He knew what she implied with her cryptic comment. To his surprise, he didn't mind if she thought he was the cause of that busyness.

They chatted for a moment longer, then Rachel was called by someone else and again they moved on.

As they circulated and chatted, Eli was starting to feel more and more like a third wheel. He had hoped by coming to the picnic that he would have a chance to spend some time alone with Rachel. But each time he thought they could go off for a walk somewhere, someone else called her name.

After meeting yet another *important personage,* he touched Rachel lightly on the shoulder to get her attention. "I'm taking Gracie to the house. She's beat." Obviously they weren't going to get much time alone.

Rachel glanced at him, then at Gracie who was rubbing her eyes with her fists. The man she was talking to frowned at this intrusion.

"I'll be right there," she said quietly. She touched Gracie on the cheek, gave Eli an apologetic smile and turned back to her guest.

Eli walked up a hill, past another group of people, along a path that skirted the lake on the property. When Charles had shown him around, he had limited the tour to the gardens surrounding the swimming pool. Eli had had no idea the property was so extensive.

And as he walked he thought, *Someday this will all belong to Rachel.* The idea gave him pause.

He had known all along who she was and where she had come from. But seeing her in the home she grew up in created a low-level discomfort. This wasn't where he wanted to be. Wasn't part of his future.

He thought back to the comment his brother had made that Sunday he had literally run into Rachel. *Aiming high.*

Eli laughed shortly. Ben had absolutely no idea.

Chapter Thirteen

Gracie was twisting in his arms and whimpering by the time Eli got her up to the house. She was warm, and along her neck and forehead her hair had spiraled into tight little curls.

He went up to her room and tried to lay her down, but she clung to him, her face all screwed up.

"You are a silly girl, aren't you?" he said as he cuddled her close. "Do you want to go to bed?"

She pouted and shook her head, her curls bouncing on her shoulders. "No bed. No bed."

"Okay. I get the message." He went back down the large, wide stairs and then down a hallway, trying to find a place where he could sit with her. He passed a large room that held a desk and some chairs and ducked inside.

It looked like this was the room Rachel had commandeered as her office. Papers were strewn over the desk and floor in, what seemed to him, a most un-Rachel-like manner.

He dropped into a large, deep leather chair with a sigh

of relief. He had been on his feet since four o'clock this morning, switching a shift with another doctor so he could be here. The anticipation of the event had been somewhat dulled by the reality. He had known Rachel would be busy, but at the same time, when she'd invited him to come, he'd had visions of them strolling the grounds, talking, finding out more about each other.

Not the small talk and chit-chat that Rachel seemed to excel at, with him as an onlooker. Gracie sniffled a bit, then settled into the crook of his arm. He stifled a yawn himself, then, giving in to the impulse, let his head fall back as sleep drifted over him.

Rachel slipped into the house, listening for Eli and Gracie. The kitchen and hallway felt cool compared to the growing warmth outside. Normally she wouldn't dare to leave in the middle of things. Normally she would be ordering staff, talking to people, all the while keeping an eye on the caterers, on the food supply, making sure no one was neglected. But this time, thanks to Reuben and Anita, she wasn't nearly as exhausted as in previous years.

And, thanks to her assistants, she had dared to duck out of the meet-and-greet and find out where Eli had gone with Gracie. They weren't upstairs, or in the formal living room, or in the family room. She heard a faint snuffling from the study. It was the sound Gracie made when asleep.

She pushed the door open farther and saw the back of Eli's blond head resting on the chair. As she walked into the room, she was arrested by the sight of this tall, lean man asleep in her father's favorite chair, Gracie curled up in his arms.

Eli looked curiously vulnerable. His hair had slipped

over his forehead and his narrow features, relaxed in sleep, looked even more appealing than when he was awake.

She had to resist the urge to brush his hair back from his face. To let her fingers trace his sleeping features. She sat down in the chair opposite, content, for now, just to watch.

Then Gracie jerked in her sleep and Eli's eyes opened suddenly. He looked around as if disoriented, blinking a few times. Then he saw Rachel and he relaxed back against the chair.

"Sorry about that," he said quietly, shifting Gracie into a more comfortable position.

Rachel got up and gently took the limp child from his arms. "I'll put her to bed."

He gave her a lazy smile. "And I'll stay here," he said, his voice still husky from sleep.

Rachel walked slowly up the stairs, her mind trying to absorb the switch in her relationship with Eli. Things were moving quickly and she couldn't keep up.

Don't analyze. Let go.

She took her time settling Gracie in her bed, covering her properly. She checked the baby monitor to make sure it was on. Part of her wanted to stay up here, to think, to try to figure out what was happening.

But overriding her natural caution was the desire to be with Eli. Alone.

Eli had moved to the leather couch when she returned, but he was awake. She could have sat on the other chair. Maybe she should have. But the promise in his eyes pushed aside her second thoughts and made her curl up in the other corner of the couch, facing him.

And to her surprise, for the first time all day, she felt as if she could truly let go. She didn't need to think and plan.

"Did she settle okay?" Eli asked, his voice a gentle rumble.

"She barely even woke up."

"You don't need to rush out there and schmooze with anyone else?"

She shook her head. Reuben and Anita had it under control. She could really get used to this. No decisions, no pressure. Just visiting and now, time alone with Eli. Something she had thought about since she saw him come on to the grounds.

"I can stay here for a while."

He said nothing, his eyes on her. She couldn't look away and neither, it seemed, could he. Then he moved closer to her, cupped her face in his hands and delivered on the promise she had seen all afternoon in his eyes. He pulled her, unresisting, toward him, curved his arms around her and kissed her.

Rachel's heart leaped into her throat as she slipped her hands around his neck, tangling her fingers in his hair. When he drew away, she murmured a protest that made him laugh.

"I've wanted to do that from the first moment I saw you today," he said quietly, teasing her hair back from her face.

She couldn't say anything. She felt as if this moment was suspended in time, a bubble of emotions separate from the rest of her life. It had been so long since she'd been held by a man.

Kissed by a man.

"What's happening here, Rachel?" Eli asked finally, his question bringing to life the feelings she had been trying to sort the past few weeks.

"I don't know." For a change she didn't want to analyze, plan or think. She just wanted to enjoy this moment. She was spending ordinary time with an attractive man and enjoying his company. She wanted to get to know him more. Already she had spoken with him of things she had hidden away even from herself.

She had let him into a part of her life that she didn't think she could face again.

She had let him kiss her. And she wanted to kiss him again.

And when he moved closer to her, her heart skittered and then slowed in anticipation.

"Neither do I." His fingers lingered on her face, his eyes following their path. "I just know that..." He sighed lightly, then took a deep breath. "I just know that I've never felt like this before. I didn't think it could happen."

She heard the promise in his words. The invitation to respond. "I didn't think you liked me when you first met me," was all she could say.

"Hey," he said. "That was my line. I saw the way you looked at me when I pulled up beside you at the stop sign."

"That's because you were riding a motorcycle."

"You did seem kind of sensitive about that." He ran his fingers through her hair, rearranging their waves, making light shivers dance down Rachel's spine at his touch.

She felt as if she was slowly floating upward, like a kite on a string, moving to a place where someone else had control. Yet at the same time, feeling the freedom of having someone else involved in her life.

The question echoed in her mind as she raised her gaze to his, reading the question in his eyes.

Was she ready to let go? To involve him fully in her life?

The thought made her feel a giddy combination of exhilaration and fear.

If she were to kiss him now, what would happen? Would she be moving to a place she could retreat from?

"Rachel, are you in here?" Meg's voice called out from the kitchen, pulling Rachel back to reality.

Eli caught her by the shoulders as if sensing her withdrawal. "Don't answer. Pretend you're not here," he said quietly. Then he drew her close. Kissed her again.

His action sent Rachel's heart into a dive like a kite loose from its string. Out of control. She felt as if she had let herself float too far. Had conceded the solid grounding that had kept her from letting emotions rule her life.

I can't be here was her first thought. *I can't let myself feel like this again. Who will catch me if I fall?*

"My power is made perfect in weakness."

Rachel caught the verse, wishing she dared believe it enough to let go fully. Trouble was, she knew that things did not always go the way people wanted. Thoughts of La-Reese's child flitted through her head. Gracie. Keith, dying, while she prayed long and hard.

She didn't trust her own emotions. Nor was she sure if she was ready to trust God yet. "I don't think we should—"

"Don't think we should what?"

The puzzled note in his voice almost made her change her mind. She felt as if she had led him on, but at the same time she was so unsure of her feelings. So unsure of what to do. She didn't know if she dared make herself vulnerable again. Dared open herself up willingly and knowingly.

"Do *this*," she said. Then, before she could change her mind, she called out, "I'm in here, Meg."

He lowered his arms, stepped away.

And as he did she felt a wave of loneliness and regret. What had she done?

"Have I misread the situation, Rachel?" he asked.

As Rachel held his eyes, second thoughts assailed her. He was good, kind, gentle. And her feelings for him grew stronger each time she saw him.

She just needed a bit of time to sort out her feelings. To find out where to put him in her life.

But before she could deny his bald statement, before she could tell him what she needed, Meg came into the office, holding the hand of a boy, her son Chance.

"Hey there," she said, her eyes roaming knowingly from Eli to Rachel. "I hope I'm not interrupting anything?"

"No. Not at all." Rachel smoothed her hair back from her face, then stopped, realizing how that looked. "Eli and I were just…"

"Done," Eli said, his gaze resting on Rachel as if questioning what she was doing. He nodded at Meg, then left.

Meg watched him go, then looked back at Rachel. "Okay, I sensed a heavy subtext here. You going to tell me?"

Rachel cleared her throat. Things were moving too fast. She needed to think. "You're reading too much between the lines. Eli and I…well, we needed to talk about Gracie." Not entirely true, but close enough that Rachel could say it without blushing.

She hoped.

Meg gave her a direct look, then laughed. "You look flushed."

Guess not.

"What did you need?" Rachel asked, moving the conversation to a place she could control.

"Chance needed to go to the bathroom," Meg said, her eyes holding a spark of mischief.

"You know where it is."

"Oh, he's done," Meg said with a wave of her hand. "But Jared wants to take a picture of you with Mayor Morrow."

"I think he's gone," Rachel said, ushering Meg and Chance down the hallway, through the kitchen and then out of the house, feeling a sudden urge to get out of the room where she had opened herself up to Eli.

The sun felt like liquid warmth flowing over her chilled skin. She strode away from the house.

"Are you okay?" Meg asked, catching her friend by the arm and pinning her with a steady look. "You seem flustered, which is not the calm and in-control Rachel we know and want to change."

"I'm fine," Rachel said, but she couldn't meet her friend's eyes. She was less than fine. She felt as if the solid foundations she had built for herself were slowly being eroded by God, by Eli, by life itself. She used to know exactly where she was going and where she hoped to end up. Now she wasn't sure she was even headed in the right direction.

She needed to explain to Eli why she had hesitated. Why she held back. Needed to explain her fear, and pray he would understand.

But she couldn't see him.

"Pardon me?" she said, dragging her attention from the people scattered over the garden back to Meg, who had been talking to her.

Meg raised her eyebrows. "Welcome back."

But Rachel didn't reply.

"Okay. Keep your little secrets. I was just compliment-ing you on how well things are going. And you seem to be a lot more relaxed."

Meg's voice had a heavy undertone that Rachel chose to ignore. That Meg had found her and Eli together was, well, unfortunate. She wasn't ready to bring the disparate parts of her life together yet. "I wouldn't be surprised if my organized friend even ordered this beautiful weather."

"The picnic is under control thanks to my able assist-ants," Rachel said, trying not to think of what she had done. Trying not to think that maybe she had lost some-thing precious.

She would just have to fix it, that's all.

She watched Chance scamper on ahead to where Jared sat with Luke. "As for the weather, well, I don't have that much of an 'in' with God," she said.

"But I do hear that you've been back in church."

Rachel shook her head. "Been talking to Pilar, have you?"

"We like to keep tabs on you."

"Nice to know." In spite of the warmth of the sun, she shivered as she looked around for Eli one more time. "I suppose I should go and talk to Jared," Rachel said, forc-ing a smile. "Do my part for Tiny Blessings."

"Tiny Blessings can use a positive image right about now," Meg said shortly.

Rachel turned back to Meg, her friend's oblique com-ment distracting her from what had happened with Eli. "What do you mean?"

"I'm sorry. I spoke out of turn."

But Rachel knew something was wrong. "What are you talking about?"

Meg shook her head, then seemed to change her mind. "I'm a little concerned about the agency. Jared got an anonymous letter the other day from someone who claimed that the birth records at Tiny Blessings had been tampered with up to thirty-five years back. He checked with Kelly, who was quite upset, but she didn't deny it."

Rachel frowned. "Kelly hadn't said anything about it to me."

"Of course not. She's trying to do major damage control. She found some files behind a false wall that had duplicate records showing some major inconsistencies. She doesn't quite know what to do right now. All I know is that for now it's very hush-hush." Meg put a finger to her lips as they got closer to where Jared and their twin boys were playing.

Twins had a special appeal about them, and when they were as young and cute as Luke and Chance were, a person couldn't help but smile. "I don't know how you tell them apart," Rachel said, as one of the boys raced past her, chasing a ball that Jared had thrown for him.

"I thought, because I had Luke to myself for so many years, that I would have no problem, but there are times they still catch me unawares." Meg and Jared had both been married to other people when they adopted their boys. Two years later, divorced Meg and widowed Jared learned their sons were twins who were separated at birth. For the sake of the boys, the former high-school adversaries had gotten married, and in spite of a few bumps along the matrimonial trail, they were now truly in love. Rachel had envied them their devotion and affection. But now, as she watched Meg bend over to kiss her husband and Jared smile up at her, Rachel again felt Eli's touch on her face.

She glanced around the picnic grounds once more, hoping, wishing. Her heart fluttered when she finally caught sight of Eli's blond head, his easy stance, his hands tucked in the back pockets of his jeans. He was talking to Kelly. And he was smiling at the attractive woman.

And Rachel was jealous.

At least he was still around. She needed to talk to him, to let him know how she felt.

"Rachel, great to see you," Jared said, getting up from the blanket he had been sitting at with one of the twins. "I hope you don't mind having a few pictures taken."

Rachel pulled her reluctant attention back to Jared, who was taking a camera out of his bag. "No. No, that's fine. I don't mind." She disliked the hesitant, breathless sound of her voice. Meg seemed to notice, as well, but Rachel refused to catch her curious gaze. "Where do you want me to be?" she asked.

"Hey. There's Kelly. We can do one with the two of you instead of with Mayor Morrow."

Jared led the way, and Rachel had no option but to follow.

She drew in a long breath as she approached Kelly and Eli. But when Eli looked up at her, he wasn't smiling.

She obediently posed with Kelly, pretended to be talking to her while Jared took pictures. Chance and Luke got into the picture, as well, representing the children helped by Tiny Blessings.

"So, Kelly, while I have you here," Jared said, "I was hoping you could tell me a bit more about some of the problems with the records at Tiny Blessings."

Kelly threw a frown at him. "There's nothing to tell."

"I heard that there were some discrepancies in the files."

"How could you have heard—" Kelly looked at Eli, then at Rachel, then Jared as if trying to connect the dots. "Did Ben tell you something?" she asked Eli.

Eli shook his head. "About what?"

Kelly turned back to Jared and seemed to make up her mind. "Yes, there have been some problems, but right now we don't want a lot of false stories getting spread around. We're still investigating and that's all I can tell you." Kelly seemed suddenly tense. "Please, Jared, I can arrange for something later on, but for now, this needs to be kept quiet." Her gaze ticked over Meg, Rachel and Eli, almost pleading with them. "Please. Right now we just don't have the manpower to deal with any panic that might come from false rumors being spread. So if you could keep this quiet, I would appreciate it. We are talking about a thirty-five-year history here. You can only imagine how many people could be adversely affected by false rumors."

Jared held her gaze as if testing her sincerity. "I can keep it quiet for now, but I'm not going to let this die, Kelly."

"Of course not. But until we have more information…"

"Don't worry. I'll keep it quiet."

"As I'm sure will everyone else here," Rachel said, reassuring her with a light touch on her arm. Meg nodded, too, but when Rachel turned to Eli, she saw he was walking away.

Her chance was gone.

Chapter Fourteen

"You should look at getting this sanded down and refinished," Ben said, tapping his foot on the floor of Eli's house. "It's quality stuff."

"That's the next project once these rooms are all done," Eli said, grunting as he dropped an armful of scraps into a box in the middle of the room. They had just finished putting up the drywall in the last room of the house. All Eli needed to do now was call in the tapers and then the painter, and the upstairs would be finished. Ben's daughter, Olivia, was staying overnight at a friend's place, so Ben was free to help.

"So why the big push?" Ben asked, brushing the white residue of the drywall off his pants. "You've been working pretty steadily on the house, but you've never asked for my help in the evenings before." He stopped, then nodded. "Or does it have something to do with a certain Rachel Noble?"

Eli kept quiet, knowing that anything he said would be misinterpreted by his brother. He swept up the rest of the scraps and dropped them into the box.

"I heard that you were quite the cute couple, hanging around the grounds of the Noble estate."

Ben wasn't going to quit, Eli realized. "I don't know about the cute part, but yeah, we spent time together."

"She's quite a catch, don't you think?" Ben asked as he gathered up his tools.

"I try not to think these days," Eli returned, picking up the box. "It gets me into trouble."

Which wasn't entirely true. Since the picnic, he hadn't been able to get a number of things out of his mind. Since that moment in Rachel's office, he had felt as if he'd been pushed back, set aside. Many times in the days that followed, he'd been tempted to phone her, to stop by the house.

But he had resisted. He had opened himself up to Rachel, had thought she had done the same. But then, just when he practically told her exactly how he felt about her, she had stopped him cold. *I don't think we should.* Then why had she allowed him to kiss her?

And why was he still thinking about her? He had resolved to put her out of his mind. He was thankful that he had this house to work on. It kept his hands busy so he wouldn't have to try to figure her out. He had cared for women before, but something about this one had made him willing to put aside his well-laid plans. Had made him willing to act like a fool.

"Thinking is overrated, as is dating," Ben said in a dry tone as he followed Eli down the stairs and out the back, where Eli set the box of scraps in the bed of Ben's truck. Ben dropped his toolbox on it, as well, then turned, leaning back against the open tailgate. "You haven't spent time with any women for a while. What's with this one?"

Eli swiped at the dust on his pants. He didn't feel like

talking about Rachel, but he also knew Ben wasn't going to quit. "I'm not sure."

"You like her?"

Eli waggled his hand in an unsure motion that he knew was insincere. If he didn't like her, why was she taking up so much of his thinking time?

"I know it's not a guy thing," Ben continued, "but you want to talk about it?"

Ben was his brother, but talking about Rachel would suddenly make everything a little more real, and, by extension, a little more unsure. So he did what any man would do when he didn't want to talk about something too close to his heart—he changed the subject.

"I heard something about Tiny Blessings at the picnic. Kelly mentioned your name. What do you know about those duplicate records she found?"

Ben scratched his head, the dust from his hand powdering his dark brown hair. "She just told me that she found inconsistencies between the official records and the ones she found behind a false wall we took down."

"Why didn't you tell me about this? You know I've been trying to find out more about my own parents."

Ben pressed his lips together. "And you know how I've felt about that. Mom and Dad gave you everything, Eli. I don't care about my birth mother. She gave me up and that is that. I wish you would do the same, especially because your parents are gone."

"Your mother also signed a 'no contact' agreement," Eli said, his frustration with his adopted brother growing. "She didn't want any connection with you. But I have memories of my parents. I know what they looked like even though Mom and Dad would never talk about them."

"You know they did that because it always made you upset."

Eli said nothing to that. He and Ben had discussed this before and they always ended up going in circles, with Ben vigorously defending Peggy and Tyrone and Eli feeling as if he was on the outside of the Cavanaugh family once again. It had taken him a number of years after he was adopted before he felt like he was truly a part of the family, and even then his memories of his own parents and their tragic death often interfered, tied in with the guilt of being the only member of his family left.

"Jared at the *Gazette* seems to know more," Eli said finally. "He asked Kelly about it, but she asked us all to keep quiet."

Ben sighed. "I'm sorry I didn't tell you about the records. I didn't think it was necessary. I thought you were over all that."

"I don't know if you ever are," Eli said quietly. An image drifted into his mind. Rachel leading him down a gallery that held pictures of her family going back generations on either side. She was rooted. Grounded. She could tell people where she came from. Eli wasn't a snob, but somehow, having the biological portion of his ancestry wiped out made him feel as if he had less than other people.

He loved Peggy and Tyrone. He loved that they had taken him in and put up with his rebellion as a youth. He knew it pained them that he didn't go to church anymore.

But at the same time he couldn't wipe out his memories. Didn't want to.

"All I can tell you, Eli, is that if you need to know more, I would suggest you go talk to Kelly yourself."

"I think I'll do that," Eli said.

* * *

Five o'clock the next day found him in the offices of Tiny Blessings just before it closed. He had phoned during his lunch break to schedule an appointment and had managed to do some juggling to get time off from work. He was getting good at this, he thought, as he followed Kelly into her office. Maybe, with practice, work might not take over his life as fully as it did now.

A picture of Rachel flitted through his mind and with it came a gentle ache. He should call her, figure out what she meant that afternoon at her parents' place. He just wasn't sure he wanted to know.

"What can I do for you, Dr. Cavanaugh?" Kelly asked after he declined coffee and sat down in a chair opposite her desk.

"I understand you have or had a file on my biological parents," he said, pulling himself into the here and now.

Kelly shook her head. "There's not much, but we have a little. It is the same thing we gave your parents, the Cavanaughs."

"Was it one of the files that was tampered with?"

"Not that we can see. It appears to be on the level."

Eli felt a momentary letdown. Since getting the pictures from the Cavanaughs, he had hoped there might be more that had been held back from him. Like any child with other parents, he felt as if part of his life had been taken away when they died. Getting whatever he could would make them more real to him.

"Can I take it home?"

"Though your file was not sealed, we don't like them to leave the office. I can give you photocopies, though."

Kelly excused herself, and while she was gone, Eli got

up and paced around her office. She had pictures of babies and young children all over the walls. Some of them were faded, obviously from the time before she took over. He wondered if there had ever been a picture of him and Ben on this wall.

Five minutes later she was back with the file and a manila envelope. "I put all the information in there. We can compare it to the original file contents if you want to double-check to make sure I've got everything."

"I'd prefer to look at it at home," Eli said as he took the envelope. It felt too light to be holding information on six years of his life. "Thanks for this, Kelly."

She stood at her desk, her fingertips resting on her blotter. "You're welcome. I'm glad I could help you so easily." She drummed her fingers lightly. "I probably don't need to remind you, but I will anyway. What you overheard at the picnic, please keep it to yourself. It will come out eventually, but for now I need some time to figure out how to proceed."

"I've no reason to spread it around," Eli said, suddenly impatient to be gone.

As he left the office, he tucked the envelope in his leather jacket, hopped on his motorcycle and took off for home.

Once there, he put on a pot of coffee, threw a frozen pizza in the oven, settled at his desk and started reading. The first part of the file was straightforward. His parents' names. Blanks for their address. No known relatives. No next-of-kin to notify. He double-checked the papers from Tiny Blessings, but as Kelly had assured him, things looked straightforward there.

He turned the paper over and found a newspaper clipping he had never seen before. He felt his stomach flip as he saw the picture of the vehicle his parents had been in. The accident that he barely escaped from. In spite of the passage of time and his acceptance of his parents' deaths, he felt anew the helpless anger he had experienced with God for taking them away.

He reread the article and the police report. Nothing new here.

He skimmed over the information about the car's registration and insurance. A phone number that had been disconnected and an address of an apartment that had only been rented for a couple of months and nothing beyond that. No one knew his parents' destination. The police had not been able to find next-of-kin in spite of notices put in papers both here and where his parents had come from.

He glanced over the newspaper article again. The paper surmised that they had been in Virginia vacationing, judging from the tent, sleeping bags and cooler of food packed in the car.

Eli looked at the date of the paper and frowned. Vacationing? In October? He had been six years old. Shouldn't he have been in school?

He jotted down the date, then turned to the last piece of paper in the file. It was a photocopy of a photocopy of a scrap of paper he had never seen. He held it up, squinting to read what looked like a scribbled note, a list of names and places, some of which were referenced in the report.

Then a name stopped him. Lisa, Brad and Eli G. He read it again as a vague memory teased his mind and it solidified. *G* was for Giroux. He instinctively knew that. But why?

He flipped back through the police reports. Nothing on

Giroux there. Then he sat back in his chair with a sense of unease.

The name made him uncomfortable. Almost afraid. As he mulled the name over in his head, a picture came to his mind. He was five years old. His mother and father were kneeling down in front of him. Frowning. Saying the name. *Eli Giroux.*

He got up and paced around his desk, came back to the file. He read the papers again. And again.

Then, on a whim, he turned his computer on, hooked onto the Net and did a search on the name. He got a number of hits, but nothing that jumped out at him. Of course, the accident had happened almost 27 years ago. No newspaper would have archives that far back.

He scrolled through the lists anyhow, checked out anything that seemed to make a connection. He did another search and added in the date of the accident, minus one year. The year he was five.

He spent the next hour refining his search, digging. He couldn't let it go, because all the while he worked, the name and the fear that accompanied it would not loosen its grip.

Finally he found something. The name Eli Giroux on a personal blog. It was posted by a man also named Eli musing about old neighborhoods. He talked of where he lived and a neighbor who had come and gone so mysteriously. They had a little boy, Eli Giroux. The man remembered it because his parents had taken a picture of the two Elis. Then, suddenly, the family had gone without telling anyone. It was the first mystery in his life. The posting meandered a bit, moving on to other things.

Eli sat back, his heart a block of ice in his chest as a

memory pushed up into his consciousness. A sunny day. Someone's backyard. His mom taking a picture of him and another boy because they had the same name.

Murky pictures formed and disappeared. A house. A swing set. Eating a Popsicle and chasing another boy. Eli.

Swallowing, he hit the man's e-mail address and sent him a quick note asking for more information.

Suddenly restless, he got up, snagged his jacket and went out the door. He had to get away. He jumped on his motorcycle and headed out, letting the wind push away the uncertainties.

When he came back, an hour later, there was a mail message for him. He hesitated to open it, unsure of what he would discover. He looked at the subject line. It could be nothing. It could be everything. He clicked it and started reading.

When he was done, he realized he had started something he couldn't stop until it was finished.

"But I have to see Dr. Cavanaugh," Rachel said, laying a damp face cloth on Gracie's face. Since the picnic two days ago, Gracie had been alternately cranky and listless. Rachel suspected she might have caught something from one of Meg and Jared's twins. Meg had called Rachel yesterday, saying that Chance had a runny nose and a fever. She was concerned for Gracie, and now, it seemed, her concerns were justified.

"I realize that," his secretary said. "I am in the process of rescheduling all his appointments for the next few days. I'm sorry, but he was called away on a family emergency."

Rachel thanked the woman, then hung up, wondering what family emergency Eli had been called away to, and wondering what she should do about Gracie.

"Wanna drink," Gracie said, rubbing her eyes with her hands.

Rachel poured her a glass of juice, then sat down with her on a kitchen chair and cuddled her while she drank it down.

Rachel set the cup on the table and gently rocked the child, singing softly to her. She didn't know what else to do. Gracie had been fussing all morning, and though her temperature wasn't very high, Rachel couldn't help feeling concerned.

Rachel pressed a gentle kiss to her sister's head. "I wonder where Eli is," she whispered, wishing he would make one of those unscheduled stops that had annoyed her at one time.

Funny how quickly things changed. Not so funny how much she wanted to talk to him. To explain what she had felt that day of the picnic. Again and again she had replayed the scene in her mind, wishing she could have said what she really wanted to say. She wanted to explain her caution, but to do that would be to show how vulnerable she felt around him. A no-win situation.

She brought Gracie back up to bed and laid her down for an afternoon nap. Gracie didn't protest, which showed Rachel just how ill the girl was. Usually Gracie fought her naps with a quiet tenacity that could make Rachel frustrated.

Now Rachel wished Gracie would display a little more vigor.

A few minutes later sleep finally claimed Gracie, and Rachel quietly left the room and made her way downstairs to her office. She read through a report from the financial department of the Foundation, jotted a few notes for Reuben to follow up on and made a few phone calls.

She tried to phone Eli at home, then on his cell phone, but both times she only got his answering machine.

Meg was busy. Anne had only a few minutes to talk. Pilar was out and not answering her cell phone. Rachel's father was away from the hospital room.

Rachel felt alone.

On her way down to the study, she met Aleeda.

"You look tired, Rachel," she said. "Why don't you go out for a bit? Let me watch Gracie for you."

Rachel glanced back over her shoulder as if to make sure that Gracie was still sleeping. It sounded so tempting.

"Take your cell phone along with you. You need to get out a bit," Aleeda urged. "Gracie's just sleeping. She'll be okay."

Rachel knew she was right. Since the picnic, she hadn't been able to forget about Eli. Instead she had plunged herself into work and taking care of Gracie. They went on walks and picnics on the grounds. She worked in her office until her eyes burned, doing busy work that didn't have a deadline, but that she had taken on just to keep herself from thinking. Still, being in the room where Eli had kissed her had brought the memories up again and again.

She did need to get out. To put other thoughts in her mind.

"Okay. I'll be back in an hour," Rachel said, then left.

Rachel slowed down as she came near the street where Eli lived. She hadn't been planning to come this way; in fact the whole reason for the trip was to try to forget about Eli. Yet she had found her way toward this part of town. His secretary had said he was gone anyway.

But Eli's motorcycle was parked in front of his house in the shade of a sweeping elm tree.

Rachel spun the wheel before any second thoughts claimed her attention. She had been mooning long enough. She needed to get this straightened out once and for all.

She cared for Eli, knew he cared for her. In her heart, she knew she simply needed to tell him what held her back. Why she was hesitant and, yes, fearful to step into another relationship. He would understand when she explained to him. She should have much sooner, but she had held her resentment, her sorrow so close to her for so long, it felt unnatural to let it go.

But she knew this was what she needed to do.

They were both adults. This should be simple.

She parked beside the motorcycle and got out, looking up at the two-story Colonial. The brick house had freshly painted buttery yellow shutters and trim. The house's welcoming look made her curious to see the inside. As she walked up the winding brick walk, she noticed that while the exterior of the house had been finished recently, the yard was in need of work.

A large cardboard box sat to one side of the front door, half full of scraps of wood, drywall, pieces of plastic, nails and other building refuse. It looked as though Eli had been working on the interior of the house, as well.

The grass was trampled-looking, and a few marigolds nodded in the front flower bed alongside a pink rosebush that had gone wild. The house would look even more homey with some landscaping. As she was imaging what plants she would put in the brick-edged flower bed, the door opened.

Eli stood in front of her, unshaven, his shirt open, carrying a box and looking so much like he had the first time she saw him in the park, that she felt a moment of déjà vu.

"Hey, Rachel, what brings you here?" He paused in the doorway, looking at her, his face holding no expression.

"I was just out for a drive and thought I would stop by. I saw your motorcycle, so…" Rachel put the brakes on her runaway words before she started babbling. Though this was a spur-of-the-moment decision, she didn't need to sound like an idiot.

Eli nodded, his expression serious. He shifted the box in his hands and, as he did, a piece of paper fluttered onto the sidewalk.

A photo, Rachel realized as she bent over to pick it up.

Eli held out his hand to her. "I'll take that," he said, his voice rough. "It's garbage."

Rachel caught a tone in his voice that made her glance once again at the photo in her hand. A young boy of about five flanked by a woman and a man. The man had the same lean features Eli did now.

"Are these your parents?" she asked. "Your biological parents?"

Eli caught the photo out of her hand and flipped it into the box. "They were," he said, and dropped the shoe box into the garbage bin.

"Why are you throwing them away?"

Eli didn't answer. Instead he turned his back on her and walked up to the house. At the door he paused and looked back over his shoulder. "Are you coming in?"

His terse invitation was hardly inviting. This Eli was a stranger to her, and she didn't know if she wanted to spend time with him. She knew she had been vague with him and had let an opportunity to fully open up to him slip by— but surely her mistake wasn't unforgivable?

He misread her hesitation. "I know the house isn't as tidy as it could be. Ben and I have been doing some fixing that I had to put on hold while I went down South." He scratched his chin with his fingers, his nails rasping over his whiskers as he stifled a yawn. "I just got back."

Rachel chanced another look at him, and this time noticed the lines of fatigue around his mouth and eyes. And the motherly part of her, that Gracie had teased out, felt a moment's empathy.

"Sure. Just for a moment. I don't want to leave Gracie with Aleeda for too long," Rachel said as she followed Eli through the front entrance, past the bright and cheery living room to what she supposed was the dining room. Thankfully, Gracie was a safe topic that concerned them both.

A lone table sat in the center of the hardwood floor, two folding chairs flanking it. Through the French doors of the dining room, Rachel could see a yard edged with shade trees. A small building was tucked into one corner of the yard, a miniature replica of the house. A playhouse.

She glanced around the house while Eli was busy in the kitchen adjoining the dining room. In spite of the lack of furniture and pictures on the wall, the house exuded warmth and welcome. The large windows let in abundant light, enhanced by the high ceilings.

This house could be a home in a way her modern and stark condo loft never could, Rachel thought with a twinge of regret.

"How is Gracie?"

"She was fussing all day today," Rachel said, sitting down on the chair, her eyes drawn, once again, to the playhouse in the yard. "I think she's got a bit of what Chance, Meg's little boy, had. Probably just a cold."

"Do you want me to stop by and have a look at her?" Eli, asked, seeming suddenly concerned.

Rachel felt a moment's annoyance. As soon as she mentioned Gracie's name, his attitude did a hundred-and-eighty degree change.

"That's okay. I rescheduled an appointment with you for the day after tomorrow."

"You are keeping a close eye on her, aren't you?"

Rachel heard the stern tone in his voice and couldn't help but bristle. Then she relaxed as she recognized it for what it was: concern for a child who was medically fragile. A child they both, in spite of what had come between them of late, cared for.

"I am," she said quietly.

Eli handed her a cup of iced tea and sat across from her. He kept his eyes on the chilled glass in his hands.

Rachel took a careful sip, wondering how she was going to bridge this sudden gap—no, make it chasm—between them.

Straightforward was usually best.

"Eli, about the other day. At the picnic. I just want to say I'm sorry. I wanted to talk to you but I was scared."

"There's nothing to talk about," he said, cutting her off. He looked up at her then and there was a sadness in his gaze that cut her more deeply than what he had said. "You and I…" He shook his head as if negating the possibility.

Rachel felt as if he had hit her in the stomach. She tried to regain her bearings. She had come here ready to tell him what she had never told anyone before. And now he was practically telling her not to waste her time? What had happened? What had changed? How had her hesitation that day caused this hurt she saw in his eyes?

She felt as if she was teetering at the very place she had almost plunged into. She took a deep breath, caught her balance and stepped back.

And then there was nothing more to say.

She gently pushed her glass away and stood. She avoided looking at him, all the while keeping a tight rein on her emotions. She wasn't going to cry in front of him. Not now. She took a careful step away from the table and walked toward the front door, praying that she wouldn't fall and embarrass herself.

The door opened just as Rachel got there and a tall man with dark hair strode in. A young girl of seven skipped alongside him. They both stopped short when they saw Rachel. The man frowned, then looked past her as if trying to figure out where she had materialized from.

"Is Eli in?" he asked.

"He's in the dining room." Rachel poked her thumb over her shoulder. She really wanted to leave, but politeness kept her standing where she was.

"I'm sorry. I'm Ben Cavanaugh," he said, holding out a large hand. "His brother. This is my daughter, Olivia."

The young girl gave her a tentative smile. Rachel forced one in return. She had never felt less like smiling, making small talk, meeting the rest of Eli's family. She returned Ben's handshake. "I'm Rachel Noble," she said.

Ben's smile lit up his face. "Rachel. I'm so glad to meet you at last."

Eli had talked about her enough that there was an "at last" to their meeting?

Ben held her hand a moment longer, then glanced past her. "Hey, brother, you never told me she was so good looking."

"Rachel was just leaving," Eli said quietly.

Had he spoken in anger, Eli's quiet denunciation might have been easier to deal with. But this unemotional dismissal of her cut Rachel to the core. She could have been an unwanted saleswoman trying to hawk brushes or plastic-ware for all the concern he seemed to express at her exit.

"Eli is right," she said, avoiding Ben and Olivia's surprised looks. "Nice to meet you."

Rachel walked past them, out the door, down the sidewalk and, she felt, out of Eli's life.

Chapter Fifteen

"You never told me how gorgeous she was," Ben said, as Eli watched Rachel back her red sports car out of the driveway. "Or that she drove such a wicked car."

Ben glanced at Olivia. "Do you want to watch some television?"

Olivia's eyes grew wide at the unexpected treat. "Yes, please," she said, and scampered off to the living room before her father could change his mind. Ben turned back to Eli.

Eli caught the back of his neck with both hands. He didn't need Ben hanging around analyzing his life. He had done the right thing. He knew he had. When he had seen Rachel on the step, the expectant thrill he felt at her presence had surprised him. But what he had discovered this weekend had pushed that expectation aside.

"I didn't tell you much because I didn't know what was going to happen," he said simply.

"Well, it looked like something happened. She left here on the verge of tears. What did you say to her?"

"Nothing."

"She came here to visit you and you said nothing? How dumb do you think I am?"

Eli sighed and looked at his brother, so different from him.

"So why did you come?" he asked, hooking his thumbs in the belt loops of his jeans. Ben's timing was terrible. Eli wasn't in the mood to visit with his brother. Not now.

"I wanted to know if you managed to talk to Kelly about your file."

Eli frowned. Where had that come from? "I thought you figured I should stay out of that part of my life."

"Let's go to the kitchen."

Eli knew he wasn't going to get anything from his brother until they were alone, so he led the way to the kitchen, Ben following him. He poured his brother a glass of iced tea, hooked his foot around a chair to pull it up to the table, dropped onto it.

"So spill."

"There was a fire last night at the Tiny Blessings office."

"What?"

"I was driving by and saw the flames. I haven't had a chance to talk to Kelly to find out what happened. I don't know how extensive the damage is, but I was hoping that you got what you needed before the fire."

Eli rocked back in his chair. How ironic. Had he waited, he might have been saved a lot of trouble and heartache. Had he waited, his parents' file might have been destroyed.

"I got a copy of the complete file from Kelly the other day. But now I wish I hadn't. Just like you suggested."

"So what did you find out, Eli?"

Eli sighed, then went for it. "The parents I thought were

so great were driving here because they were on the run from the law. I found out that they weren't the wonderful, amazing people of my memories. They were simply common crooks."

Ben almost spat out his tea. "What?"

"I tracked down some information, did some digging. My name wasn't Eli Fulton, it was Eli Giroux. When my parents had the car accident, they were on the run from the police in another state. They were wanted for embezzlement and robbery and for questioning for a bunch of other unsolved petty crimes." Eli shook his head and swigged down the rest of his iced tea in one gulp. Then he pushed his cup back and forth between his hands, his movements agitated.

"Does Rachel know?"

"I couldn't tell her, and why should I?"

"Because when you talk about her, you get this sappy look on your face. And when you look at her…" He lifted his hands as if to say, *You know what I mean.* "I think you love her."

Eli gave the cup another shove. "I do. But what am I supposed to do about that? This house isn't ready. I've still got debts. She comes from a very rich family, and my own parents, I've just discovered, were crooks. Quite the family tree I'm offering her."

"Don't be such a reverse snob. I don't think that would matter to her."

Eli laughed shortly. "You obviously haven't seen the Noble Plantation. And she doesn't know my family's background."

"I don't think you give her enough credit," Ben said sadly.

"Well, for now, I don't have much to give her, period."

He looked up at his brother. "Cut me some slack, okay? I do care about her. A lot. But right now my life is a mess and I don't want to go into a relationship with all this stuff hanging around me."

Ben leaned over and clapped his brother on the shoulder. "Eli, life is always going to be a mess when you let other people in. You are way too devoted to this so-called plan of yours. I don't think you should wait until you've got all your ducks in a row. I think you need to give this your best shot. I think she's worth it."

"You're full of advice, Ben, but I know that you're not ready for another relationship."

"That's *my* life, brother," Ben said, with a warning note in his voice. "Yes, I lost Julia and it hurts more than I can say. God gave me a raw deal when that happened and I still don't trust Him, but I don't want to see you waste an opportunity."

Eli just nodded, still unsure. Ben didn't know Rachel. Or her life.

"C'mon, honey. You have to drink something," Rachel said, coaxing Gracie. But she turned her head aside, tucking it against Rachel's chest. Rachel could hardly hold the little body, she was so warm.

Rachel had tried to lower her temperature using the horrible method Eli had shown her, but while it had given the child momentary relief, her temperature had spiked again. Rachel glanced at the telephone, wondering if she dared phone Eli.

But when she did, she thought of the cool note in his voice, how easily he had dismissed her yesterday. She almost laughed at the irony of it all. She had avoided Eli because she didn't want to hurt again.

And now, because of him, a slow steady pain had permeated her life. She missed him. Wanted to be with him. But he had pushed her away. She should have kept her heart whole. Should have listened to her own advice.

Rachel got up and started walking, rocking the little girl who lay listlessly in her arms. It was eleven in the evening, and in spite of her self-talk, Rachel was alone and afraid. She didn't know where to turn. Again she had that feeling of being out of control that she'd had when she was with Eli.

"If I settle on the far side of the sea, even there Your hand will guide me, Your right hand will hold me fast."

The words of a Psalm that Reverend Fraser had read when Rachel had gone to church slipped into her mind. She held them a moment.

Did she dare put herself in God's hands? Let go? She'd had to learn so many lessons in letting go and, to her surprise, they had come easier than she'd thought.

But this? To put her feelings and love for this child in the hands of a God who had let her down so cruelly in the past? To let go of Eli, as well? Because she knew that what she felt for him was deeper than what she had felt for Keith. And the thought frightened her.

Gracie jerked in her arms. Then her arms flung out to the sides as her eyes rolled up and her head snapped back.

Rachel had no more time to think.

She ran to the phone and with shaking hands punched in 911.

Fifteen minutes later she was running behind the paramedics as they pushed the gurney holding Gracie's convulsing body through the large glass doors toward the emergency room.

They turned down a hallway. Rachel tried to follow them, but was suddenly restrained. "Miss, you can't go there."

A nurse was talking to her, and Rachel whirled around, about to fight her off. She had to go, had to be with Gracie.

"They need to work and you'll get in the way. Your little girl is in good hands," the nurse was saying.

The words fell like loose pebbles into Rachel's mind. She understood but couldn't grasp them.

"Stay here. The doctor will come and let you know what is happening." She was young and shorter than Rachel, but the hands that held her were surprisingly strong.

Rachel threw a glance back to where they had taken Gracie, but the gurney and the paramedics were gone.

She felt suddenly lost as she looked around the busy room. She didn't know how she had gotten here. She vaguely remembered the rocking ambulance, the two men hovering over Gracie, working on her, their voices crisp as they volleyed instructions back and forth. Instructions she could not decipher but that had increased the panic that bubbled in her chest.

The nurse gently but firmly led Rachel to a low counter with chairs on one side and a bank of computers on the other.

Rachel mechanically went through the list of questions. No allergies. Medications. Told the nurse again who Gracie's doctor was.

As she answered she felt some of the panic sift away. She had a job to do right now and she concentrated on giving the nurse the best information she could. As if by answering the questions calmly and saying each word precisely she could help Gracie, could remove that blank look from her sister's face, could restore the color to cheeks the color of her mother's best white damask tablecloths.

They were finally done. Rachel declined the offer of water from the nurse. "When can I go see my sister?" Rachel asked.

"I'll find out what is going on." The nurse got up and quickly walked to the ward, leaving Rachel fighting a latent anger. Complete strangers were working on Gracie, able to see her at will, and here she was, her own sister, barred from seeing her.

Rachel paced the floor, watching the minute hand crawl over the clock face. She kept her eyes averted from the other people in the waiting room. Her mind could not take in their pain and worry, as well.

Finally the nurse returned. "She's stable now. They just transferred her up to pediatric ICU."

Rachel felt a cold weight settle on her chest. "I thought you said she was stable."

"She is. But she needs to be monitored closely." The nurse gave her a careful smile. "She is okay. For now."

"For now?"

"I can take you to her, if you want."

"I do." Rachel followed the nurse, focusing on putting one foot at a time in front of her. They got into a stuffy elevator, and Rachel looked at her hands. The nail polish she had painstakingly applied the day of the picnic was getting chipped.

In fact she realized she was wearing a stained, oversize T-shirt and baggy cargo pants that had seen better days.

A couple of weeks ago she would never have been seen in public with less than a perfect hairstyle, perfect manicure and one of her many power suits.

Right now, she didn't care.

The elevator pinged, the doors slid open and Rachel followed the nurse down the hallway to a set of double doors. The nurse walked up to a cubicle with a window and spoke to the nurse behind the desk there. The doors magically opened and Rachel was directed to a sink, where she was instructed to wash her hands.

"You won't have to gown up," the nurse told her as Rachel dried her hands off.

The nurse led her to an open room that held four small beds surrounded by banks of monitors. Only one other one was occupied, but Rachel had eyes only for Gracie. She looked like a tiny doll on the bed, wearing a hospital gown that had slipped off one shoulder. Rachel focused on that, shifting it carefully up, moving it so the snaps on the shoulder would not press into her delicate skin.

She couldn't look at anything else.

She was far too aware of the tube inserted in Gracie's mouth, the hiss of the respirator that breathed for her, the bleep of various monitors that measured her life. The plastic lines that snaked from her chest and her arm through other machines to bags of fluid that hung over her bed that sustained that life…

A few hours ago she was a tiny body that Rachel could cuddle and hold close. Now she was connected to equipment, hindered by the paraphernalia.

A familiar panic rose in her chest. She couldn't be here. She couldn't see this tiny body laying helplessly in this organized confusion of tubes and monitors. She couldn't watch this little girl's life seep away.

Just like Keith's had.

There wasn't enough air. They had taken all the oxygen out of the air and given it to her little sister. Rachel felt a dark curtain slowly lower over her vision and she reached blindly behind her. Her hand caught the back of a chair and she lowered herself into it.

She inched her hand through the side rails of the bed. When she found Gracie's hand, she slipped her fingers around it, careful not to dislodge the oxygen monitor clipped to Gracie's thumb.

The momentary contact with her hand fanned an ember of hope.

"My power is made perfect in weakness."

The passage from the Bible settled into her mind and Rachel repeated it again and again, wishing she could remember the rest of it, wishing she had spent more time reading the Bible, and praying. She was so out of practice, and, for now, it was the only thing she could do.

Would it help? It hadn't the last time she had sat beside the bed of a loved one, sending up earnest prayers for recovery.

But even as the thought slithered through her mind, a part of her did not accept it. She had felt God's presence the other Sunday and since then. She could not deny His existence. It was His world and she knew it. All her life she had heard what her position in this life was—and that was to serve God, not the other way around.

She laid her head against the cold metal of the bed rail, her eyes on the too still and quiet form of her little sister, feeling utterly helpless, exhausted and out of control. And she started to pray.

Eli paused in the doorway of pod C of Pediatric ICU, his heart heavy. As soon as he had found out about Gracie he had rushed to the hospital.

Before he had come to the room he had read the chart, double-checked the medication and discussed Gracie's care with the on-call pediatrician. All the tests had been ordered and she was going to have another CT scan in the morning. For now, she was unconscious but stable.

At the moment, his greatest concern was for the pale woman clinging to Gracie's hand, her head bent over a book barely illuminated by the morning light coming through the curtains behind her.

The charge nurse told him Rachel had been here all night and had only left Gracie's side once, to make a couple of phone calls. It was now seven o'clock in the morning. Shift change.

He felt as if he had no right to talk to her, after what he had told her the last time they saw each other. But since then he had fought the urge to phone her. To explain what he had discovered and how it had spun his life around.

He was the son of criminals. This information starkly reminded him of a moment in his past. The parents of another girlfriend had told her to break off with him when they found out he was adopted. They didn't know his family background. Didn't know where he came from.

Well, he knew now, and though it was years ago, he still could feel the sting of that betrayal. Even worse, he knew the girl's parents were right to warn her away from him.

Yes, he was older now. Yes, he was wiser. Yes, he held a solid place in the community.

But in spite of all that, he couldn't help but wonder if the same weakness flowed through his veins. He had read enough patient histories to know that often a child would become what their parents were.

When Rachel had come to see him at his home, he had been trying to absorb the information. To figure out where to put it in his life. To find out his biological parents weren't the good, kind and decent people he had created in his mind was to sweep away the very foundation of his life.

Did he dare to hope it wouldn't matter to her, when it had mattered so much to him?

He banked his thoughts, focusing on why he was here. He wasn't on duty for another hour, but a patient of his lay in Intensive Care. And a woman that he cared for more than he had ever cared for anyone else was crouched beside the bed.

He walked quietly into the room, his eyes glancing over the monitors, checking, measuring. As he came near the bed, Rachel looked up from the book she had been reading with an almost hungry desperation.

It was a Bible.

Her face was drawn and he could see she had been crying. The pain on her face drew him. He stood beside her, trying to treat her with the same level of compassion and caring he did the parents of his other patients. Even though all he wanted to do was pull her up into his arms, comfort her, hold her close…

"Is she going to be okay?" Rachel looked up at him, then away.

Had he imagined that yearning look on her face?

"She's stable for now," Eli said carefully. "We've ordered a CT scan and we're waiting to hear back from the lab on her blood work. We've upped her seizure medication a bit, just to be on the safe side."

"What caused this?"

Eli shook his head. "We don't know. With Gracie and

her condition, seizures are a very real threat, especially when her system is so stressed."

"Will she come out of it?"

"Overall, Gracie is a very healthy little girl. Her lungs are good. Her heart is strong. I believe she will."

Rachel looked at him as if she didn't believe him, then back at the Bible. "I've been reading about how God tells us to trust in Him and He will give us the desires of our heart. Do you believe that?"

Eli sighed as he glanced over at Gracie, then back at Rachel. "I don't know what to believe, Rachel. I just know that we are doing whatever we can for Gracie. And I'm willing to put my trust in the technology we have to keep her alive."

Rachel gave him a weary smile. "I put my trust in that once before and it let me down."

"When Keith was here?"

She nodded, then straightened, wincing.

As she got up from the chair a nurse came over to Gracie's bed.

"The charge nurse tells me you've been sitting here for hours," Eli said. "You want to go and get some coffee? Give Wendy here some space to work?" Eli tugged gently on her hand. "Gracie will be okay while we're gone."

"I'll let you know immediately if anything changes," Wendy said, looking up from the monitor she was adjusting. "Things look okay for now."

Rachel glanced down at Gracie, then nodded. "That would be nice," she said quietly.

Eli took the Bible from her and set it on the table beside Gracie's bed. Then he led her out of the room and down the hall, past the heavy double doors that led to the

ICU ward and along a hallway to a parents' lounge. He was relieved to see it was empty this morning.

Rachel dropped into a soft leather couch and laid her head back while Eli put on a pot of coffee. As it burbled and hissed, he sat down in a chair across from her, his elbows resting on his knees, watching her.

Rachel pushed her hair back from her face. "I must look like a train wreck."

Her hair was tangled and her clothes were far more casual than anything he'd ever seen her in before. She wore no makeup and her face was drawn and tired.

"You look beautiful." The words slipped out before he could stop them.

Rachel lifted her head, her puzzlement showing in the faint frown on her forehead. He didn't blame her. Two days ago she had come to him, opened her heart to him. In response he had virtually kicked her out of his house—and then been blasted by his brother for doing so.

But what else could he have done? His own life had been tossed about, his memories stolen from him, tarnished and rearranged by what he had found out.

He didn't know who he was anymore, where he belonged. How could he, in turn, ask someone like Rachel to be a part of a life he didn't understand?

Because for a brief and wonderful moment, he had considered it.

She stretched and dug into a pocket of her pants, pulling out an elastic band. "Can you tell me what is wrong with Gracie?" she said quietly as she twisted it around her hair, moving the topic of conversation to their mutual concerns. "I know it was a seizure, but what caused that?"

"I can't give you a whole lot more than that. With a child like Gracie, her health can be unpredictable. We talked a bit about that before you started taking care of her."

"Was it something I did? Should I have kept Chance away from her? I keep going over and over all the possibilities and wonder if maybe I shouldn't have…"

Eli reached over and touched his finger to her lips, stopping the flow of guilt that spilled out of her mouth. "Rachel, don't do this. Gracie was prone to seizures before she got this cold. She could just as easily have sailed through it with only a runny nose and a cough. Or she could have had this seizure when she was perfectly healthy. We'll know more when we get the results of the blood work and do a CT and possibly an MRI to find out what is happening."

Rachel only nodded, avoiding his eyes. "So for now it's a matter of wait and see what the test results bring. And pray."

"I'm surprised you are even willing to consider that," Eli said, remembering her pain when she had opened herself up to him in his house. Since that day he had struggled with his own reactions. He had done to her the very thing he was afraid would be done to him.

He'd be left behind. Be hurt by someone that he cared for.

What else could he have done?

You sought her out. You made her think something was happening between the two of you.

And now? He wasn't sure what to think. His once well-ordered and controlled life had been turned upside down. He needed time. But now, sitting across from Rachel, he realized that he still needed her.

"I didn't used to pray. I thought it was a waste of my time."

"So what changed?"

"My life." She gave him a careful smile. "I thought I was in control of everything, and for a while I was. I had the right job and the right place to live and the right life. It was my way of dealing with the loss of Keith. And, maybe in some strange way, figuring that if I did it all exactly right, God wouldn't punish me with something bad happening."

"But now Gracie is ill."

Rachel sighed. "Yes. And I'm scared. And sad. I'm torn between wishing she had never come into my life and praying that she never leaves. It hurts and I don't like it. But in a way it's a good hurt."

"How can you say that?"

"Because when I hurt, I know I'm alive. After Keith died I shut everyone out and shut my emotions off. I didn't want to be in a position to be hurt like that again. You see, part of my problem was that I blamed myself for Keith's death. If we hadn't fought, he wouldn't have taken off angry and wouldn't have been hit by that drunk driver. We fought about his motorcycle, you know…" She stopped and gave him a trembling smile. "The last things he heard from me was me ragging on him about that machine. If we hadn't fought—"

"Rachel, don't think that. It wasn't your fault."

"I know that now, but for years, I thought it was. I thought I didn't deserve to have a relationship because I didn't know how to take care of it. Then Gracie came into my life." Rachel smiled, took a breath. "I was afraid of her, too. Because she was so fragile. I thought if I didn't love,

I wouldn't hurt. That was why I held back from you at the picnic. I was afraid. And I'm sorry I was afraid."

"Rachel, please don't apologize for that." His heart ached at the sorrow in her voice, at what she had told him. It was a gift of trust.

Rachel was about to say something, then stopped, her lips quivering. Eli could stand it no longer. He moved closer, drew her into his arms.

She pressed her face into his neck, her tears warm on his skin. "I'm scared, Eli. I'm so scared. And I don't want to feel this way again. I prayed so hard for Keith and it didn't do any good—" Her voice broke and she clung to him, her hands clutching his coat. "I am scared to pray again, but I don't know what else to do."

Chapter Sixteen

Eli stood at the end of Gracie's bed, watching her chest rise and fall with the jerky rhythm of the respirator. The sight of a child hooked up to machines always hit him deep and low.

He was off today, but here anyway. Out of habit he glanced at the monitors. No change.

On the one hand it was something to be thankful for. On the other, it meant she had now been unconscious for twenty-four hours. And he had no idea why. He also had no idea how to pull her out, other than to wait.

And pray.

He wished he could. At one time he had been able to, but that had been so long ago. He had seen so much happen since then. He had been the bearer of sad news to parents who, like Rachel, had hovered at the bedside of a child, hoping and praying for the best.

He had watched his brother suffer when his wife died of cancer.

"How is she doing?" Rachel's voice broke into his thoughts.

"The same." He turned to her, his heart softening at the hint of fear in her eyes, the vulnerability she wore so easily now. Before he could stop himself, he feathered a strand of hair back from her face, let his hand linger for the briefest of moments. "Did you sleep?"

"Just a little." Rachel smiled up at him, then slowly rotated her neck, as if trying to work the kinks out of it. "Are the girls gone?"

"You just missed them leaving."

Pilar, Meg and Anne had come to visit and had, with Eli's help, managed to talk Rachel into laying down for a while. They had stayed at Gracie's bedside and Eli had heard them praying for the little girl. Well, whatever it took…

"I'm so glad they came."

"You're lucky to have such good friends."

"Or blessed. I'm so thankful for their prayers." Rachel moved to Gracie's side, gently stroking her cheek. "Does she feel me touching her?" she asked.

Eli heard the plaintive note in her voice and it drew him to her side.

"Some part of her does acknowledge touch, and hearing. But we have no way of measuring that."

"Will she wake up? Will she be herself when she does?"

"I wish I could tell you that everything is okay," Eli said, feeling more helpless around this patient than he had for a long time. "Gracie has her own set of problems, but we are doing whatever we can."

To his surprise, she caught his hand in hers.

"I'm glad you're her doctor," she said. "I'm glad you're here."

He squeezed her hand, appreciating the contact, wishing he could cure Gracie for her. Wishing he could infuse the right medication into Gracie's IV to pull her out, to make her come back. Wishing he could do all that to put a smile back on Rachel's face.

He wanted to tell her about his parents, explain why he had pushed her away. But before he could speak, a nurse came to the doorway.

"Rachel Noble? Your parents are here."

Disappointment mixed with relief flowed through him. He had to catch his breath, make new plans.

Rachel squeezed his hand even harder, then dropped it. "Thank the Lord."

"We do have a limit of two visitors at a time," the nurse warned Rachel. "So you will have to leave if they come in."

"I understand." Rachel glanced back at Gracie as if loath to give up her vigil.

"I'll stay here until you come back," Eli said.

She looked up at him, her features softened by sleep, her eyes glistening with unshed tears. "Thanks."

When she left, Eli turned back to Gracie, his hand touching the curls that lay on the pillow. And he felt a need rise up in him. A need to speak.

To pray.

Would it do any good?

Would it do any harm?

"Please, Lord" was all he could say as he curled his hand protectively around Gracie's face. "Please, Lord."

He stayed by her bed until he heard Charles and Beatrice's hushed voices and Rachel's low response. He left the pod and met them outside in the hallway. Beatrice was in a wheelchair, Charles pushing her. Beatrice held Rachel's hand. They looked almost as tired as Rachel did. But Eli could see in their eyes a steely determination that gave him a confidence he didn't feel in himself.

He briefly described what they would see, preparing them. He told them what the staff were doing for their daughter, and said he wished he could give them better news.

"We believe you are doing whatever is humanly possible," Charles said, laying a comforting hand on Eli's shoulder. "Why don't you take Rachel away for a few minutes so we can visit Gracie."

"I'm sorry, Mom," Rachel said quietly, bending over to kiss Beatrice. "I'm sorry you had to come home to this."

"Baby, don't you even for one moment think this is your fault," Beatrice said, cupping her daughter's face in her hands. "I'm glad you were around to help her. This could just as easily have happened in her sleep." Beatrice pulled Rachel's head down and pressed a kiss to her forehead. "You go and have a cup of coffee. You look as if you could use a break."

Rachel gave her a weak smile, then Eli lead her parents into the room.

She was leaning against the wall when he came back, her head bowed. When he approached, she looked up and gave him a wavering smile. "You don't have to come with me."

"Yes, I do," he said.

She pushed herself away from the wall and trudged down the hallway through the silent swing of the large double doors and toward the family room. A young couple got up from the couch when they came in.

"Please, don't leave because of us," Rachel said.

"My husband and I were leaving anyway," the woman said with a huge smile. "Our baby is coming home tomorrow and we want to get some rest."

"I'm so glad for you," Rachel said. "I pray that things will go well for you at home."

"Thanks for that." The young man draped his arm across his wife's shoulders and gave her a quick hug. He smiled down at her and she laid her head on his shoulder.

Eli felt a touch of jealousy. They looked content, happy. It was what he had wanted for himself, what he had thought, briefly, that he and Rachel could have.

As the door sighed closed behind them, he caught Rachel watching them, her face holding a look of yearning.

"I'm glad they can go home," she said softly. "Be a family." She sighed, then busied herself rinsing out the coffeepot. "Do you want any coffee?"

"No."

She glanced over her shoulder, then slipped the pot back into the coffee machine. "I didn't either, but thought you might."

"I've drunk enough for the day."

"Some hot chocolate?"

"No thanks."

She nodded, then sat on the couch, fidgeting.

"Gracie is okay for now," Eli told her. "Your parents are there now and the nurses are always right there."

"I know." She looked up at him, patting the seat beside her. "Can you please come and sit down here so I don't feel like you are towering over me?"

He hesitated, sensing a change in the atmosphere. He wasn't sure he wanted to have this conversation. But as he looked down at her upturned face, his gaze was caught by her soft brown eyes. He lowered himself to the couch beside her.

"I need to tell you something, Eli." She looked down at her hands as she twisted a ring around her finger. It was a simple stone, pale green. Eli realized then that it was the only jewelry she ever wore.

To his surprise, she took his hand in her own. "I had a visitor this afternoon—your brother Ben. He told me about your biological parents. What you found out about them."

Irritation flared up in him. "I didn't know my brother was such a font of information."

"He came looking for you, but I was the one who wanted to talk to him." Rachel stopped, her finger pressing lightly on the scar on his hand. A reminder of his past. "I wanted to ask him about you."

"Why?"

"Because that day I came to visit you, I came to tell you that I had made a mistake at the picnic. Like I said, I was afraid to let someone else in my life. Losing Keith was a hard thing, but those days that I didn't hear from you were almost harder. It hurt, Eli, and I don't want it to hurt anymore. And I wanted to know why you stayed away. I thought maybe your brother would know."

Eli thought of her parents sitting at her sister's side. So normal and ordinary. Solid, respectable citizens. The kind of people he had thought his own parents were. Their life was well ordered and stable. A life like the one he had hoped to have for himself before he felt ready to let someone else into his life.

"I had a plan for my life," Eli said. In spite of his own reservations, he curled his fingers around her hand. He didn't want to let go. "I was going to buy a house, fix it up, put money aside, pay off loans. All neat and tidy. I wasn't supposed to meet someone I cared about for another year or two." He laughed lightly, then looked at her. "You came early."

Rachel's dark eyes widened but she didn't look away. "What are you saying, Eli?"

"I care for you, Rachel. More than I've ever cared for anyone else. You've turned my life upside down. But since I found out about my parents, I don't know what to think, what to feel."

"What do your parents have to do with anything?" she cried, her hand tightening on his.

"I thought they were these wonderful people…I thought—" He stopped, wishing he could lay it out all neat and tidy, like a report, but he couldn't. And Rachel was looking at him with such compassion that he knew that he had to tell her in whatever way he could.

"I grew up knowing I had other parents," he said, gazing down at their joined hands. "I grew up in a wonderful, loving home, but I always felt, because I had other memories, that I was on the fringes of my adoptive family. Ben had come to them as an infant without memories, and I know there were times that Mom and Dad didn't quite know what to do with me. Like I told you before, we never talked about my biological parents. Never mentioned their names. When I found a box of photos in Mom and Dad's house of me and my parents, I felt angry and betrayed."

"The pictures you were throwing out?"

"Ben pulled them out of the trash," Eli said with a rueful smile. "Interfering brother that he is. I was angry with Mom and Dad Cavanaugh when I found the pictures, thinking they had been holding something infinitely precious from me. I'm sure they had their reasons."

"Did they know the truth about your parents?"

Eli shook his head. "No. I think it was like you said that one day in the park. Maybe they thought they were doing me a favor. But I had created a dream family around my biological parents. I'm pretty sure I'd often thought, when the Cavanaughs were disciplining me, that if only I were with my real parents, they would be better. So when I got the pictures, I felt as if I had connected to a very important part of my life, a better part. Then, when I found out what my parents really were—" he lifted his shoulder in a slow shrug "—I felt betrayed a second time. I knew I had hurt Mom and Dad with my anger and rebellion about my biological parents and it was all over a fantasy. A dream. I feel like I've made such a mess of things."

"But life isn't orderly and tidy, is it," she said, reaching up and touching his cheek. "I found that out when I started taking care of Gracie and a certain doctor laid out the rules in no uncertain terms. I had to let go of a lot of control—and I don't do that very well." She glanced at the door, as if trying to look past it to Gracie. "I've spent a lot of time the past few days praying, trying to figure out what God wants of me, and I don't know. I don't know if He's going to spare Gracie or take her away. I fought so long and hard with Him over Keith, thinking that if I just prayed hard enough, things would happen the way *I* wanted."

"They don't, do they."

"I used to be in control of my life. But I had to let go of that. I am trying to find God again."

The conviction in her voice called to a buried part of Eli's own life. A part that his parents had nurtured in him by bringing him to church, reading the Bible with him, encouraging him to develop his own devotional life.

He had pushed that aside. He had found out, in his work, that often God didn't make sense. God let some children die and others live. Eli couldn't figure it out. God didn't come all neat and tidy and packaged.

And he had pushed God aside because of that. God didn't fit in his well-ordered life.

Well, that life wasn't so well-ordered anymore.

He now sat beside a woman he had come to care for in a way he never would have thought possible.

"So how do we do this, Rachel?" he asked, unsure of what direction to take now.

"I read a quote by Irving Townsend this afternoon, that to open up to other people is 'to live within a fragile circle easily and often breached.' I know I was afraid of that. Afraid to let you in. But it started with Gracie." She gave him a careful smile. "I'm still afraid of what will happen to her, but I'm learning to let go, to put her in God's hands. Because I know that as a perfect parent, He loves her more than I do. And I'm learning that sometimes the pain is worth the loving."

Eli touched her face with his fingers, marveling at this amazing woman. Then, without thinking or weighing or measuring, he leaned closer and kissed her. She clung to him.

"I'm glad you're here, Eli," she whispered again as she tucked her head under his chin.

He was, too. They had only just begun to explore this new relationship. No, he wasn't ready for it—but, he suspected, neither was she. It was happening and they would have to deal with it as it came.

The door opened and they sprang apart. It was the charge nurse and she looked harried.

"Eli. Come quick. Gracie's in distress."

Chapter Seventeen

Rachel sat perched on the edge of the couch in the family room, clutching her mother's icy cold hands. Charles paced the room behind them as Reverend Fraser, sitting across from them, read from Psalm 46, his deep voice creating a cocoon of comfort.

"'God is our refuge and strength, an ever-present help in trouble. Therefore we will not fear, though the earth give way and the mountains fall into the heart of the sea, though its waters roar and foam and the mountains quake with their surging.'"

Rachel let the words rest on her weary and tired mind, holding her up. *Ever-present*, she reminded herself.

"Charles, will you join us?" Reverend Fraser asked.

Charles stopped, then with a nod sat beside Rachel.

Reverend Fraser took Beatrice's and Charles's hands, Charles held Rachel's, Rachel held Beatrice's, closing the circle.

Reverend Fraser began to pray. He interceded for Gracie. Prayed for Eli who was even now frantically working to save the little girl's life. When he prayed that, if it be His will, He take Gracie, Rachel almost cried out in protest.

But she felt her mother's and father's hands holding hers and she knew that she had to let go of Gracie.

When they were done, she looked up at Reverend Fraser. "Thank you for coming," she said quietly. "It means a lot to have you here."

He smiled at her. "We are family, Rachel. We help each other."

"I know and I'm thankful for that." She got up from the couch, feeling suddenly restless. She knew God was watching over her sister, but she wanted to watch, as well. But the charge nurse had kept them away, telling them that Eli and the nurses needed no distractions.

She stood by the door, looking out the window at the double doors of the ICU. Beyond them she could see a nurse running with a cart toward Gracie's room, and her heart knocked against her rib cage.

What was happening?

Dear Lord, please keep her with us. Please let us keep her a little longer.

She stayed by the doorway as if keeping vigil, praying and praying.

"She's going into another seizure." The nurse's voice was clipped as she held Gracie's spasming body down.

"Increase the Valium," Eli said, one eye on her blood pressure. "B.P. is dropping," he said. "Give her a fluid bolus." Another machine went off.

"Oxygen levels dropping, as well," another nurse said.

Eli snapped out orders, his eyes moving from one monitor to the other, watching, measuring, planning for various scenarios.

Gracie had crashed once and they had managed to stabilize her, but now her seizures were like waves, one after the other.

Status epilipticus was the technical term.

"C'mon, Gracie," he whispered, looking back at her. "Stay with us. Rachel needs you. We all need you."

A few tense moments followed the changes they had made as they watched and waited. And Eli prayed—formless, half-coherent prayers. Prayed for strength, prayed for wisdom and pleaded that this little girl would be allowed to stay.

"B.P. is climbing," one nurse said.

Eli nodded and watched, ready to respond should anything change.

"Oxygen levels are rising," the nurse said, just as he noticed it himself.

Relief sang through him as he realized Gracie had turned the corner. She was going to pull out of this.

Eli waited a few moments longer, making sure that she was stable. Then he left to tell Rachel and her parents.

His hairline was damp with sweat and his back was tight from bending over the bed. He was tired and worn, but exhilarated at the same time. This was why he had become a doctor, he realized. These moments when all his training came together and he could save the life of a child.

He caught himself. No. He had only been used by God. Ultimately it was God who was in control. God who had saved her life.

It was a humbling way to look at his work, he realized as he trudged down the hallway to the family room. But it was also freeing. He didn't have complete control. He only had to do what he could. God was in charge of it all.

Rachel saw him coming and was the first one out of the room. She ran up to him, catching his hands in hers, her face silently pleading with him.

"She's going to be okay."

"Thank the Lord," Rachel breathed. She clung to him, then burst into tears.

"She looks good," Rachel whispered, standing beside Gracie's bed. Her parents had left an hour ago. Rachel looked exhausted, her face drawn in the subdued lighting of the hospital room, but she told Eli she didn't want to leave until Gracie was settled for the evening.

"She'll be fine now," Eli said, standing behind Rachel. He placed his hands on her shoulders and Rachel leaned into him.

"Thank you," she said, angling her head up to look at him. "You're an amazing doctor."

"I'm just a doctor," he said. "Which definitely has its humbling moments."

Rachel pulled away from Eli and bent over her sister, placing a gentle kiss on her head. "Have a good sleep, precious one," she said. She sighed, then turned to Eli. "I'm ready to go now."

He reached past Rachel and stroked Gracie's cheek with one finger. "Thank You, Lord," he whispered. Then he slipped his arm around Rachel and together they walked out of the room and down the hallway toward the elevators. One came quickly and they stepped inside.

As the doors slid shut behind her, Rachel yawned and tunneled her hands through her hair. "I feel like a grub," she said.

"You look wonderful," Eli said, tousling the hair she had just tried to rearrange.

"Flattery even at this time of night?"

"Why not?" Eli looked down at Rachel, then dropped a quick kiss on her lips.

"Is this how you treat all your patients' relatives?" she asked with a smile.

"Just the ones I really care about." He caught her by the waist, holding her gaze. Her expression became serious as the implications of what he had said sank in. He swallowed, then took a chance and went one step further. "Just the ones I love."

Rachel lifted trembling fingers to his cheek, her gaze still locked with his. "And how many are those?" she whispered.

"Only one." To seal his promise, he pulled her close, and slowly, gently, kissed her.

Rachel returned his kiss. Then she drew away, her eyes shining. "I love you, Eli Cavanaugh. I didn't think I'd be able to say that."

He smiled, then kissed her again. And again.

"Are you getting out?"

Eli glanced back over his shoulder. The elevator had stopped and the doors were open. An older man and woman stood in the hallway of the main floor watching them with benign expressions on their faces. A few people who walked by slowed down, smiling at the picture they made.

"Sorry," he muttered, an embarrassed flush warming his neck as Rachel drew away from him.

"This is nothing to be sorry about," the man said, as he held the door open for his wife, smiling at them both. "Love is always something to celebrate."

Rachel giggled, then caught Eli by the arm and pulled him out of the elevator.

"Take care," the woman called out as the doors closed behind them.

Eli sighed. "Well, that was romantic. Somehow I didn't think I would end up making declarations in an elevator. With an audience." He looked around the hallway. Though it was late evening, the hospital was still alive with nurses and orderlies intent on their work, the night cleaning staff doing their job and relatives of patients wandering around, waiting.

"What are you looking for?" Rachel asked.

"Someplace discreet and private where we can talk properly."

Rachel caught him by the front panels of his lab coat and standing on tiptoe, kissed him quick and hard. "I love you, Eli. And I don't care who knows or sees us. I don't care about proper and I don't care about having things all neat and tidy. I don't care where you came from and I don't care where we're going. Not anymore. I just want to be with you."

Eli shook his head and curved his arm around her waist. "So do I. But I would prefer to have some ordinary conversation without onlookers."

Rachel leaned against him and sighed. "*Ordinary*. I do like the sound of that word."

"It does have a nice ring to it, doesn't it," Eli said.

"So where should we go?"

"How about your parents' place? It's not that far."

"That's not so private," Rachel said, a frown wrinkling her forehead.

"Are you kidding? There must be at least sixty rooms in that place."

"Only fifty-four," Rachel protested. "And some of those are servants' quarters."

"Pardon me," Eli said with a laugh. "But I'm sure we can find someplace quiet to talk in one of those fifty-four rooms."

"I guess we could," Rachel said, slipping her arm around Eli as they left the hospital together.

"Pick a flower?" Gracie asked, toddling over to where Rachel sat beside her parents' swimming pool and dropping a couple of wilted pansies in her lap.

Rachel pushed her sunglasses to the top of her head and smiled at her sister as she took the flowers. "Looks like you've been busy, little one."

Beatrice sat nearby in the shade of an umbrella, her foot up on a stool. The cast had come off a week ago, but she had been counseled to take it easy for a few more weeks. So Rachel had offered to work out of her parents' home for a while longer. It wasn't the best system, but it worked. Anita and Reuben were wonderfully capable and had proven to be an efficient team, giving Rachel a little more time to spend with her parents and Gracie.

"When did Eli say he was coming?" Beatrice asked, laying her book on the glass-topped table beside her.

"He had hoped to be here between three and four." Rachel took one of the pansies Gracie had given her and tucked it in her hair. It was now three-thirty, but she wasn't worried. Eli always gave her a broad range of time to allow for emergencies.

The noise of a car engine coming up the drive made Rachel frown. "Are you expecting company?"

"Not that I'm aware of. Do you mind seeing who it is?"

"Aleeda can come and let us know."

Beatrice laughed. "You are getting far too good at delegating, my dear. Go and see who it is."

"All that delegating you've been nagging at me to do has made me a spoiled, lazy girl." Rachel stretched her arms over her head and stood. "But I'll go find out who dares to intrude on our privacy. C'mon, Gracie. You come with me. Mom can't jump in after you if you decide to go for a swim in the pool."

Gracie obediently took Rachel's hand and toddled along beside her.

The inside of the house was cool after the warm sunshine as Rachel and Gracie made their way to the front entranceway. Just as they entered the main foyer, the large front door opened and Eli stepped inside.

A wave of pleasure spiraled up inside her. "Hi, there! How did you get here? I didn't hear your motorcycle."

Eli bent over and kissed her gently, then picked up Gracie. "I have another mode of transportation."

"Is something wrong with your bike?" Rachel pulled away and walked to the front door to see for herself.

"Just wait, Rachel," Eli called out.

But Rachel was outside already and looking at a silver car parked beside her red one, puzzled. "Who did you borrow that from? Ben doesn't have a car like that."

Eli sighed. "He doesn't and I didn't. Borrow it, that is."

Rachel was truly puzzled now. "So why…?"

"Look, Miss Nosy, I traded in the bike for this."

Rachel stared dumbly at the car, then realization dawned. "You got rid of your motorcycle!"

"See. That's what I love about you. Gorgeous *and* quick." Eli tossed her a teasing smile.

"But why?"

"Well, someone once quizzed me on the suitability of a pediatrician riding a motorcycle."

"That someone sounds dangerously pretentious," Rachel said, still trying to match this car with the man she had come to know and care for.

"Be careful, darling," he drawled. "You're talking about the woman I love."

Rachel walked to the car and touched it lightly, as if to make sure it was real. Then she turned back to Eli, a tiny fragment of happiness lancing her heart. "Why?"

"Because I know how you feel about motorcycles and, as much as I hate to admit it, you're probably right. If I'm going to settle down…" He stopped, tilted a smile her way.

"Settle down? As in get married?"

Eli heaved a sigh, settled Gracie more firmly in his arm, then pulled Rachel to him in a one-armed hug. "I wanted to make this all official and proper, but you messed this up, you know. Rachel, I want to marry you."

Rachel's chest could not contain her heart. Happiness and love and thankfulness danced around trying to find an outlet.

So she cried.

"Hey. I'm not that bad a catch, you know," he whispered into her ear as he drew her close.

"I love you, Eli Cavanaugh." She pulled back, cupped his beloved face in her hands and pulled him down for a kiss.

"Eli. Rachel," Gracie cooed, clapping her hands as if catching their happiness.

"You got that right, little one," Eli said. He turned back

to Rachel. "I was hoping to talk to your father first, then go get a ring, then try to find a private place on this cramped estate of your parents' and do this all proper without an audience..." He shrugged.

Rachel placed her finger on his lips and laughed. "I'm glad you didn't. I'm glad Gracie could be here. After all, she was the one who brought us together."

Eli's expression grew serious. "I'm glad she did, Rachel. I thank God every day for what has happened in my life because of that. Because of you."

Rachel didn't think she could take any more happiness. "You are a gift, Eli Cavanaugh." She gave him a hug. "Now, let's go find Mom and Dad."

And together they walked back through the large double doors of the Noble family plantation, looking for the rest of their family.

Dear Reader,

We like to think that we are in control of our lives. However, we all know that people, events and just the day-to-day stuff of life conspire to show us that this is fiction. I still struggle with control, though my husband and I learned a lot about letting go when we took in our first foster child. This blessed child had multiple handicaps, and his care was a challenge each day. Like Gracie in the story, he had cerebral palsy, but on top of that he had a stomach tube for feeding and was on oxygen and medication for seizures. God had entrusted this child into our care, but, at the same time, we had to learn important lessons in letting go. Not only of control and plans for the day, but also of life. When he passed away, after four and a half years in our care, we faced another aspect of letting go. But we also found grace and strength in Christ's love for us.

The verse that I used in the front of this book is incribed on his gravestone. It is a reminder to us to realize that God can use our weaknesses. He is the master planner, and His plans are the best.

I love to hear from my readers. You can write me at either Carolyne Aarson, Box 114, Neerlandia, Alberta, T0G 1R0 or e-mail me at caarsen@telusplanet.net. If you e-mail, please put "Brought Together by Baby" in the subject line so I know it is a valued letter and not spam.

Carolyne Aarsen

Pilar Estes works closely with Detective
Zach Fletcher to uncover who left a
baby boy ON THE DOORSTEP,
coming only to Love Inspired in September 2005.
For a sneak preview of this book by Dana Corbit, please
turn the page.

Pilar parked a few buildings past the agency office and backtracked. A gust of wind fluttered her bangs and whipped her long black ponytail over her shoulder. She crossed her arms over her blouse, wishing she'd worn a sweater.

With her gaze on the sidewalk cracks instead of the narrow former bank building that for thirty-five years had housed Tiny Blessings Adoption Agency, she mentally ticked off a list of her other duties before the big Labor Day weekend. A home visit to schedule. An introduction to plan between prospective adoptive parents and a darling toddler with special needs.

"Lord, please help me not to be distracted from my work today," she whispered when her thoughts flitted back to her own needs. Reflexively, she pressed her hand against her lower abdomen, as if she could protect the fragile organs inside. The minor cramps that had brought her into the doctor's office in the first place squeezed again, taunting her.

"Please help me to stay focused," she restated, knowing full well she should have been praying for healing or at least acceptance of God's will.

That she couldn't manage more than that today only frustrated her more. She'd never had patience for weakness in herself, and she wasn't about to go soft now just because she had an upcoming appointment at the hospital.

If she'd been looking up from the sidewalk, she might have noticed it sooner, but Pilar was already halfway along the walk before she noticed what looked like a giant lidded picnic basket resting on the building's wide porch.

She jerked to a stop. Images of ticking explosives and chemical contaminants flashed in her mind's eye, before her good sense returned. She'd been watching too many television action shows. This was Chestnut Grove, she had to remember. Until a few months ago, she could have referred to her city as a real-life Mayberry, until her own agency's horrible discovery of falsified birth records. That was inexcusable. Still, bombs and other big-city mayhem hadn't taken the bus out to Richmond's suburbs yet.

To be safe, Pilar approached the basket slowly, tilting her head and listening for any *tick-tick-tick*. At first, there was only silence. She snickered. Who did she think she was? Some Sydney Bristow *Alias* wannabe without the cool disguises and martial arts moves? Her bomb-deactivating skills would probably be wasted on a gift basket from grateful adoptive parents. She occasionally received baskets, though usually during office hours.

Just when she'd gathered the courage to come close and lean over the basket, a strange grunting sound had her jerking her hand back. She listened again and heard the same grunting—a *human* sound.

"Oh dear." The words fell from her lips as she lifted the lid. A pair of bright blue eyes gazed at her from a little pink face. Pilar didn't move. She couldn't. Seconds must have ticked by, but time stalled in a crystal vacuum as the baby's unblinking gaze and Pilar's frozen stare connected.

Strange how the child wasn't upset but content, swaddled in a receiving blanket and resting in a nest made of an expensive-looking blanket. But then a louder-pitched grunt splintered the silence as tiny feet kicked against the covering. The perfect round face scrunched and reddened.

"Oh, you poor little thing." Finally able to move again, Pilar dropped her purse and keys and crouched next to the basket. Carefully, she lifted out the baby and loosened the blue receiving blanket that had a race-car pattern. Since the sleeper beneath the blanket was also blue, she assumed the baby was a boy. "How could anyone have left you here like this?"

Her sudden movement and her voice must have startled him, because he jerked his hands and kicked his feet. Still, he didn't cry. Warmth spread from the small bundle through Pilar's blouse and into her heart. For several seconds she cradled the child, her body automatically rocking to a silent lullaby.

Pilar drew the side of her thumb down a perfectly formed jaw, the skin satiny beneath her touch. How pale his cheek appeared against her golden skin tone.

Instinctively, the baby turned his head toward the source of stimulation and worked his mouth in search of a meal. Pilar shifted him to her shoulder and stood.

"Sorry, sweetheart. Can't help you with that. But I am going to help you."

Balancing him against her, she crouched for her keys

and unlocked the door. She rushed inside, rattled in a way that was unlike her.

When she reached her desk, she rested her hand on the phone and hesitated. "Call the police and emergency workers first. Then Social services. Or is it Social services first?"

Did she really expect the baby to answer? She shook her head, both to answer the ridiculous question and to pull herself together. She could do this. Even if she did work for a private agency rather than Social Services, she was familiar with laws concerning abandoned children. She'd just never seen one close up before.

And now, turn the page for a sneak preview of
BETRAYAL OF TRUST,
the final book in THE MAHONEY SISTERS
miniseries by Tracey V. Bateman, part of
Steeple Hill's exciting new line,
Love Inspired Suspense!
On sale in October 2005 from Steeple Hill Books.

Raven Mahoney's jaw dropped as the sickening thud of truth slammed her with the force of a major league line drive to the gut. While she'd been playing the dutiful maid of honor and helping with wedding preliminaries for her sister Denni, she'd just missed out on reporting the press conference of the year. As far as Raven was concerned, that smacked of injustice.

From the TV screen in Denni's living room, cameras flashed at dizzying intervals. Raven could almost feel the claustrophobia she experienced every time she stood among the crowd of reporters, fighting for the chance to ask a question.

And she almost always got her chance to ask the tough ones. But not so tough the speaker wouldn't respond. She knew her success was a nice combination of her looks (especially if the speaker was a guy) and her instincts about how to ask the right questions so they sounded less intimidating to the speaker. At thirty-five, she'd gained a lot of savvy in her field and she was ready to move one step up the ladder of success.

Only, the teenybopper on the screen in front of her was getting the story, she, Raven, should be getting. Something akin to a growl rose in Raven's throat, and her predatory nature kicked in. *Enjoy the cameras while you can, little girl, because as soon as I get home, you are going down.*

Raven closed her eyes and imagined herself at that press conference. Where she wanted to be. Despite the jumble of cameras and elbows jabbing into her head, she itched to be there in the thick of things. To prove, once again, her value to the station. Ten years on the job had to count for something, didn't it?

Her chest tightened, and pressure began to build. But this time, the claustrophobia struck in the living room of her soon-to-be-wed sister's Victorian home. Being in the bosom of her loving family suddenly felt more like standing in a trash compactor as the walls inched closer and closer together until finally they squished her in the process. A familiar sentiment over the past few years. Since her mother's death, when she'd learned the truth about who Raven Mahoney really was.

In retrospect it all made sense. But the revelation only served to make her feel more like an outsider in the midst of this family—and all these years later, Mac still hadn't set the record straight. Nor had Raven. Mac had no idea she knew. And as angry as she was with him for keeping the truth from her, she didn't have the heart to confront him.

"I can't believe Matthew Strong is pulling out of the race." Keri, Raven's younger sister, married barely a year herself, to her childhood sweetheart, flopped onto the overstuffed green couch next to Raven. "I was going to vote for that guy."

"Shh!" Raven glared at her sister and turned up the volume with the remote.

"Sheesh, soo-rry."

"What's going on?" Middle-sister Denni entered the room, her eyes on the TV.

"Shh, or you'll get your head yanked off," Keri said in an exaggerated whisper.

"I'll talk if I want. It's my house. Besides, I'm the bride and everyone must cater to my whims. So there." Denni stuck her tongue out at Raven.

Raven rolled her eyes at the childish gesture, but couldn't resist a smile before shifting her focus back to the TV.

Her claws extended at the sight of the so-called reporter staring out from the screen. Kellie Cruise, an upstart and a spoiled rotten brat—way too under-qualified and inexperienced to be covering a press conference. Especially one of this magnitude. But nepotism at its finest continued to be at work for the daughter of the news director. And Raven knew if she didn't act fast, the just-out-of-college kid was going to get Bruce King's job when he retired. The job that Raven wanted. Deserved.

"What's going on?" Mac Mahoney's booming hint of an Irish brogue filled the room.

"Shh!" The three girls spoke in unison.

"Hey, now. Is that any way to speak to your father?" He scowled, but quieted, as his attention turned to the blond-haired, blue-eyed reporter who was wrapping up the "Breaking News" coverage.

"We've been told that Mr. Strong will not be answering any questions on the subject of his withdrawal. Now or ever. His decision is final and based on personal reasons which he apparently has no intention of revealing."

The camera shifted back to the studio where the white-haired, almost-retired anchor stared out at the TV audience.

"There you have it, folks. In the political upset of the year, a candidate that analysts and polls favored by a three to one margin, has withdrawn his name from the race for senate with only six weeks left until the primary." The older gentleman heaved a sigh. "To reiterate… With no warning for his supporters and no explanation, Matthew Strong has pulled out of the race for the Missouri senate."

If he'd said "And may God help us all," Bruce couldn't have been more obviously biased. It was too apparent that he had high hopes for Matthew's election to senate. No matter how much she might agree, Raven couldn't help but be a bit irritated with his transparency. Part of good reporting was remaining detached. Keeping your opinion carefully masked behind the facts and nothing else. Perhaps it was simply that after so many years behind that desk, Bruce didn't feel he had anything to hide—namely his opinion.

With a sigh, Raven switched off the set as regular programming resumed. Tense silence reigned in the room and she knew her family was struggling not to ask the question. Finally, she could take the tension no more and she shot to her feet. "Okay, yes. It's Matthew."

"Your Matthew?" Mac looked at her over half glasses.

"Yes." She rubbed her throbbing temple with the balls of her fingers in an attempt to ease the pressure. *My Matthew.* Regret for what might have been all those years ago shot through her. She hadn't allowed herself second-guesses. No regretting her decision.

She could still see Matthew's expression of bewilderment as she'd placed the diamond engagement ring into his palm and curled his fingers around the token. She'd walked away. Switched schools. And that was the last time she'd spoken to him.

Keri's voice brought her back to the present. "Wow. I wonder what his folks think of him leaving the race. He was a surefire win for his party."

Raven fingered the cell phone hooked to her waist-band. She itched to phone Ken at the station and get the scoop. The press had to know more than they were re-porting. No one pulled out of a race without giving some sort of an explanation—even a bogus one. Was there a gag order? She was tempted to make the call, but doing so now would betray her impatience to have this wedding over with so she could get on with her life. She'd been here two days as it was—long enough. Too long, actually, from the looks of things.

Matthew! Couldn't you have waited a few more days to do this idiotic thing?

Fingering a loose thread on the arm of the couch, Raven considered the new development. What could have hap-pened to make Matt give away the chance to eventually run for president?

Suspicion
of Guilt
by Tracey V. Bateman

The Mahoney Sisters

Someone wants Denni Mahoney's home for troubled young women shut down, but could the threat be coming from inside?

"One of the most talented new storytellers
in Christian fiction."
—CBA bestselling author Karen Kingsbury

*Available at your favorite retail outlet.
Only from Steeple Hill Books!*

Steeple
Hill®

LISSOGTVB

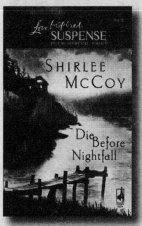

Take 2 inspirational love stories FREE!

PLUS get a FREE surprise gift!

Mail to Steeple Hill Reader Service™

In U.S.
3010 Walden Ave.
P.O. Box 1867
Buffalo, NY 14240-1867

In Canada
P.O. Box 609
Fort Erie, Ontario
L2A 5X3

YES! Please send me 2 free Love Inspired® novels and my free surprise gift. After receiving them, if I don't wish to receive anymore, I can return the shipping statement marked cancel. If I don't cancel, I will receive 4 brand-new novels every month, before they're available in stores! Bill me at the low price of $4.24 each in the U.S. and $4.74 each in Canada, plus 25¢ shipping and handling and applicable sales tax, if any*. That's the complete price and a savings of over 10% off the cover prices—quite a bargain! I understand that accepting the books and gift places me under no obligation ever to buy any books. I can always return a shipment and cancel at any time. Even if I never buy another book from Steeple Hill, the 2 free books and the surprise gift are mine to keep forever.

113 IDN DZ9M
313 IDN DZ9N

Name _____ (PLEASE PRINT)

Address _____ Apt. No. _____

City _____ State/Prov. _____ Zip/Postal Code

Not valid to current Love Inspired® subscribers.

Want to try two free books from another series?
Call 1-800-873-8635 or visit www.morefreebooks.com.

* Terms and prices are subject to change without notice. Sales tax applicable in New York. Canadian residents will be charged applicable provincial taxes and GST. All orders subject to approval. Offer limited to one per household.

® are registered trademarks owned and used by the trademark owner and or its licensee.

INTLI04R   ©2004 Steeple Hill